HE WHO WOULD WALK THE EARTH

GRIFFIN BJERKE-CLARKE

Roseway Publishing
an imprint of Fernwood Publishing
Halifax & Winnipeg

Copyright © 2025 Griffin Bjerke-Clarke

All rights reserved. No part of this book may be reproduced or transmitted in any form by any means without permission in writing from the publisher, except by a reviewer, who may quote brief passages in a review.

Development editing: Jazz Cook
Copyediting: Alicia Hibbert
Cover design: Guided by Polaris
Text design: Brenda Conroy
Printed and bound in the UK

Published by Roseway Publishing
an imprint of Fernwood Publishing
Halifax and Winnipeg
2970 Oxford Street, Halifax, Nova Scotia, B3L 2W4
www.fernwoodpublishing.ca/roseway

Fernwood Publishing Company Limited gratefully acknowledges the financial support of the Government of Canada through the Canada Book Fund and the Canada Council for the Arts. We acknowledge the Province of Manitoba for support through the Manitoba Publishers Marketing Assistance Program and the Book Publishing Tax Credit. We acknowledge the Nova Scotia Department of Communities, Culture and Heritage for support through the Publishers Assistance Fund.

Library and Archives Canada Cataloguing in Publication
Title: He who would walk the earth / Griffin Bjerke-Clarke.
Names: Bjerke-Clarke, Griffin, author.
Identifiers: Canadiana 20250155095 | ISBN 9781773637228 (softcover)
Subjects: LCGFT: Novels.
Classification: LCC PS8603.J465 H42 2025 | DDC C813/.6—dc23

For nimooshoom

"We create fictions and then we declare them natural, normal, and necessary. We won't be changing any of them until we recognize that they're just stories that can be changed."

— Harold R. Johnson

CONTENTS

PART I

1. Golden Water / 1
2. Farmhouse / 6
3. Flat Plains Sojourn / 10
4. To Rest Deep in Loam / 15
5. Forever Journey / 17
6. Dust Walk / 24
7. Burrow / 28
8. Liditz Meadow / 31
9. Snow and Sand / 35
10. Flames of Time's Arrow / 40
11. Man With the Loud Voice / 48
12. Downstream / 54

PART II

13. Township of Doufsanctville & Avaramck / 62
14. Oppidan Delirium / 69
15. Stroll / 78
16. Visitor / 81
17. Drowning / 89
18. Festival / 94

PART III

19. Hunt / 104
20. Impossible Forest / 107
21. Fixing the Well / 120
22. King of Nothing / 133
23. Imprisonment / 150
24. Children / 161
25. Involuntary Armistice / 169
26. Rebuilding the Caverns / 173
27. The Blond Beast / 177
28. Beyond the Forest / 181

Acknowledgements / 190

GOLDEN WATER

THE SUN WAS LOW as Felix Babimoosay journeyed ever forward. He had walked for several days, stopping only where he had to — hamlets, rivers and clearings when his calloused feet grew tired of walking on the flat plains. The blue sky above and the sparse greenery below left the air dry and the wind blowing strong. The buzz of distant insects and the sharp wind stung through the skies.

Several rabbits hopped in a line before the horizon — brown and white together in a flock. Even their fur did not know what time of year it was meant to be. The wind tumbled over his back, pushing him forward and nearly throwing him off balance as he went. The land with no seasons was a cruel place.

There were few signs of life on the plains most of the time, apart from insects and the rare sight of small game. Every time Felix saw a town, he wondered how people could survive so long in such an empty place, with so little to eat. Every building seemed to be a challenge to the landscape itself — with the growing number of collapsed houses he saw, Felix became convinced that no one could live longer than a few short years on the flat plains before succumbing to the elements.

At least if he died in a town, he stood a small chance of being buried — on plains, he would be forgotten by all save for the ravens that would scavenge his rotting flesh.

No one would ever know his name.

He had not been calling himself Felix Babimoosay very long, but it seemed better than any other name he had been offered before. His other names had faded into his thoughts as he pushed his feet forward and never looked back. It was the only way he knew. As long as he had been walking, he had let his destinations disappear as soon as he passed them by. If he had been sent to die, it wouldn't be long before he collapsed in a heap on the side of a dirt road — yet his feet kept moving forward as if to outlast the creeping wind on his back for a few short days longer.

He felt his throat with his hand. As he gulped, he struggled to recall the last time he had water. His eyes began to close as he walked — he fought to keep them open as he stumbled, and each time he looked again at the road, the landscape shifted slightly. The road sloped, and the trees — the few that they were — fell further into the distance. He tripped and caught himself several times until his legs finally gave in and sent him to the ground.

He lay on the dirt, wondering if these moments were to be his last, until the sound of trickling water crept through the air.

He stood to his feet, summoning the last of his strength as he found a stream ahead of him. He ran toward the water, eager to quench his thirst.

Felix knelt beside the stream and took some of the water in his hands. A migraine had settled into his temple at some point on the road, but the cool water of the stream stifled the headache into numbness. He lay on the ground and watched as the clouds were pushed against the sky. He returned often to the sight of the dancing clouds — the sky was his only companion on the road.

He stood up, ready to move on, but a small glimmer in the water of the stream caught his eye. As he knelt down beside the stream once more, the shine beneath the water became gold in his eyes — it was still under the steadily drifting currents of the stream. He thought of all the things some gold might buy in one of the towns — a proper meal, a tent, maybe even a small cabin if he were lucky — and he reached into the depths with a firm hand until his arm was submerged in dirt to the elbow. The deceptive shallow depths of the water meant that he couldn't watch what he was doing and reach in at the same time — he had to turn his head away from the stream as he dug around blindly with his hand. As he searched for the gold, flopping his hand about the bottom in search of something solid, Felix thought about how ridiculous he must look.

Felix felt nothing but dirt and rocks against the bottom but kept digging in search of the gold he had seen. He pictured it in his mind, trying to remember where it had been before he reached into the stream. Soon, he gave up and decided to remove his hand so he could see the placement of the gold once more. Maybe he nudged it during his struggle to retrieve it from the depths. As he pulled away, he felt a strange force grab hold of his arm, keeping him in place. He pulled repeatedly, trying to free himself until he realized that he was only wasting his energy. Felix paused and turned his head to the side. He remained there in strained quiet, broken only by the sound of the rushing current. His arm soon grew tired, and he struggled to keep his body upright against the water. As a chill began to set in, his arm grew numb under the surface.

As Felix fought with his weight to keep himself upright, a nuthatch landed from the sky and hopped into the water of the stream. The bird turned to Felix and then back to the water, bathing in the flowing current as it fell around a rock. Felix grunted as he pulled his hand again, trying to avoid falling into the stream. The bird turned and hopped toward him. He looked away from its gaze and tried to focus on his hand — when he grunted again, the nuthatch let out a squawk that resonated repeatedly in its throat. The bird hopped onto Felix's head and watched his hand, its beak peaking downward into Felix's field of view. It squawked louder and louder as Felix continued to struggle in the dirt. Soon, he grew irritated and swatted at the bird. The nuthatch flew away and continued squawking from the other side of the stream — beyond Felix's reach. He grunted and pulled harder as the bird squawked again. Still, the dirt refused to release him. Felix gritted his teeth and continued to pull his arm until it finally gave way, and he collapsed onto his side in the stream. The bird let out another squawk — the loudest it had made since landing beside the stream — and flew around Felix several times before disappearing into the sky.

When Felix looked upwards, he saw that the daylight had faded, and night had settled quickly into the sky. He drifted in and out of sleep and rapidly gave up on his hand — at least, he decided, until daybreak.

His sleep was filled with nothing but a feeling of damp angst that soon faded the line between waking life and dreams.

When the sun rose and the light returned, Felix couldn't be certain that he had slept at all. With his free hand, he wiped his eyes and prepared to return to the gruelling task of freeing his interned hand from the bottom of the stream. He felt his strained back and tried to move his feet outwards into the landscape. His spine straightened out with a pop and his pain was relieved.

His arm was still numb from the cold water, but it responded to his movements. He closed his eyes and a small feeling returned to his hand, allowing him to feel the mud's tightened grip from his ceaseless pulling. When he held his hand still and moved it — only gently — with the flow of the current, it sent small pieces of dirt flowing away from his wrist. After a brief, unclear remark to himself about the bizarre water of the stream, Felix began to gently twist his hand from the dirt. When the cool light of early morning illuminated into the heat of midday, Felix was finally able to gently remove his numb, frozen hand from the stream. When his fingers were free, he remembered the gold and grasped gently to retrieve a handful from the depths.

He fell back on the grass with a wide grin. He felt his sore shoulder relaxing as the hot air dried his drenched arm, returning a regular feeling to his hand. When he opened his fingers once more, he saw only dirt in his palm. He felt a wave of frustration for the endeavour but was even more happy to be free.

Felix stood up and hurried to the stream, ready to make a second attempt, when he realized that there was nothing in the stream but dirt. He walked along the stream in search of the gold, but when the glint finally appeared, Felix realized that it was nothing more than the light of the sun shining on the water. He wanted to weep at the cruel divulgence of a truth that had been hidden from his senses — though plainly obvious in hindsight — but all that came was bitter, wounded laughter that battered his gut as it rattled through his lungs.

In the silence, he heard a loud caw break through the air. He turned to see a crow bathing in the river, only to look at him and caw repeatedly. The bird hopped toward him and made another loud noise.

"Bit of a fool, aren't you?" The bird seemed to say.

Felix rubbed his eyes and watched the bird fly away. He cupped his hands and took a few swigs of water, writing off the talking bird as some sort of hallucination — it had been some time since he had found any water, and now all he could do was quench his thirst and try not to think about the filth and grime in the stream.

He lay still a while to catch his breath before rising to his feet and continuing down the road, though he wondered how many more steps he had left in him.

FARMHOUSE

FELIX'S VISION WAVERED AS HE SCHLEPPED toward the horizon under the burning heat of the sun. He found himself in one of the long stretches along the plains that was devoid of any buildings, let alone a settlement of any kind — the flat land had swallowed the hills and any form of life with them.

Any shape on the horizon had been absorbed into the sweeping fields of wheat that danced under the bright sun.

When Felix finally saw a lone rabbit prancing across the plains, he was compelled to chase the animal. He wiped the sweat from his brow and turned to face the rabbit's direction. He watched as it ran, becoming a small speck in the oceans of wheat that were draped over the landscape. Felix let his feet tumble one after the other as he walked, his mouth drooling at the thought of finding whatever had been keeping the rabbit alive — wherever it was going, it needed to eat and drink too.

He only stopped when a tall shadow eclipsed his field of view — suddenly the light of the sun was blocked, and he felt its heat leaving him. With a squint, he looked up and saw a dark shape that quelled his eyes to adjust to it as he held his head still. The curves of wood and the rust of metal faded into clarity as Felix stared, and soon the shape of a long-forgotten farmhouse was before him. He stood, wondering for a moment who had lived in the farmhouse when it had been newly built and properly kept. The door was as worn as the rest of the building. It was covered in peeling paint, and it lay hanging on rusty hinges. With a hesitant hand, Felix opened the door and stepped into the mediocre shelter of the abandoned house.

His eyes shifted to a movement near the back of the room. He turned — the rabbit sat beside him, sniffing the air. They stood for a moment, watching each other in silence. Felix slowly approached and readied his hands to grab hold of the creature. When he was only a few inches away, the rabbit sprinted, disappearing into the sea of wheat just outside the window.

He sat on the floor and looked around the room. As his stomach growled in his gut, he decided to wait for another animal to happen by the building. To turn his mind away from the anticipation, he looked over the walls that surrounded him.

The single-storey farmhouse had been a spacious shelter — livelier many long-gone years ago. Whether it was the shell of a collapsed farm or the monument of a failed settlement, the large room told of a number of people — at least five — living here in days since swept away by the unceasing wind of the flat plains. Felix sat on the floor of what used to be the living room, away from the broken glass and rested his hands on his knee — the wind that still blew strong outside sounded nothing more than a faint whisper as it whistled through the fallen windows. The silence was as unsettling as it was comforting — Felix had already grown used to the wind on his back.

The house was once full of life — now there were only the faint echoes of half-faded ghosts.

Felix stood up and wandered about the house. The other rooms of the house — three bedrooms, a small kitchen in the back corner of the house, and a bathroom that had long since been covered in a clew of slender, ribbon-like worms — were in similar states of quiet disarray. None of the rooms had doors and all of their windows were broken. The worms writhing in what had once been the bathroom sink were the only sign of life that remained in the building. He found himself standing over the worms and watching them squirm under the mould-covered faucet. He reached out a curious hand and turned the small wheel over the sink — a singular green drop landed in the porcelain, sending a small commotion among the worms below.

Felix returned to the dishevelled living room. He looked to the floor and saw the scratches on the wood where a couch used to be. He sat down where he imagined the cushions were at one time. He felt his breath return and realized that it was time to move on — he stood up and walked toward the door. As he reached for the knob, shapes danced in the corner of his eye, and he turned to find three rabbits staring back at him.

He stepped forward to chase them — one by one if it meant eating that night — as a soft rumble sounded from one of the windows at the front of the house.

Felix hurried to the door and swung it open. When he opened it, he saw the land in front of the door open so that the dirt around it was swallowed by the earth. He stepped back into the house and slammed the door, not quite believing what he had seen. He turned to the living room, and the rabbits were gone without a trace. He looked through a shattered window and saw a moat of fallen plains form around the house as everything in sight was swallowed by the onslaught of destruction. When he peered down into the pit that was left behind, he saw nothing but an emptiness that allowed for only a small glint of light near the sundering plains.

His heart sank, and he searched for an escape so he wouldn't be abandoned in the isolated building at the centre of a deep pit of fallen earth. He ran to each of the windows in search of a small piece of intact land — something to get him across the rapidly expanding depths. Desperate, he found out of the bathroom window a narrow pathway leading back into the horizon. Felix climbed out of the window, stepping over the writhing worms on the frame and jumping atop the small remains of land around the farmhouse. He stepped gently toward the path and prepared to cross the crude bridge.

Then he broke into a sprint, slowed only by the thin width of the path where he ran and the fear should his steps give way. Even still, he stumbled several times, nearly falling into the pit — Felix kept running, taking note of his disorientation only for the length of time necessary to fix his balance. Before long, he felt the ground falling — with each step, the dirt beneath began to fall as he went forward. Felix tried to hurry his step as the land fell behind him — soon after he noticed the pace of the destruction, he was forced to hop along the remaining land to outrun the falling earth behind him. With each bound potentially being his last, Felix leapt into the air and fell onto his side in the grass as the intact land of the flat plains presented itself once more.

The taste of blood was potent in his mouth as he lay on the ground, catching his breath. He pushed himself onto his back and watched the air for a moment as he felt relief wash over him. He felt his legs tingling with pain from the rush — it was a strain he hadn't noticed until he stopped running.

He turned his eyes — unable to turn his head — and he saw the three rabbits hopping off into the distance. He thought briefly about chasing them but soon realized that he should preserve his energy and keep moving.

As long as he was moving, he was alive.

When his legs were calm again and his breathing eased, Felix sat up and looked toward the house once more. Before Felix, there was nothing but the vast flat plains — the house, the pit and all traces of them had vanished. Felix took shook his head and wiped his eyes before standing to his feet. In the absence of any shelter, he could only keep moving forward — there was nowhere to go but into the horizon.

FLAT PLAINS SOJOURN

HE ARRIVED AT A HAMLET — a settlement of impossibly small size with only seven houses flanking a saloon in the centre. Felix's breath in his lungs was only half-relieved. Felix walked into the town, and the spattering of people barely glanced at him, clearly used to a steady stream of travellers. The only one who took notice of him was a man dressed in tattered rags who lay dying just outside the town. He asked for a few coins to buy something at the saloon, but Felix kept walking, too concerned with his own thirst to worry about the dying man. He stopped and turned back to see the man on the ground as other faces ignored him. He approached, counting the remaining coins in his pocket — fewer remained than he remembered. When the man looked up again, Felix removed his hand from his pocket and turned away as he felt tears well in his eyes. He tried to squint to stop them as he walked among the indifferent faces.

When he stopped for some water at the saloon, he noticed he only had money for half a glass. The other coins in his purse had been exhausted at various sojourns long since forgotten. He threw the last of his money onto the counter with a shrug. Now his pockets were dry instead of his mouth and the water in the poorly-cleaned glass was of little comfort. He tried to repel any thoughts of what may have stained the rim of his drink. If the stain carried a disease like his more frantic thoughts claimed, nothing could be done on the road. His heart pounded as he imagined dying of some horrible, untreatable sickness at the side of the road, but his throat was dry. After a few seconds, his thirst proved stronger than his fear of maladies.

Felix tried to let the water last as long as it could. He couldn't explain why except that it made the rest seem longer — as long as he was sitting in the bar, he had nothing to worry about outside.

When the bartender asked who he was, Felix shrugged, gulping down the remainder of the water anyway. The liquid poked his parched throat, only making his thirst greater. He tapped his finger on the counter to distract from the pain in his throat.

"It doesn't matter anymore," he said as he felt his mouth go hollow. "I left all that behind a long time ago. Names are meaningless things anyway. All that really matters is that I'm still on my feet — I haven't died yet and that means more to me than whatever mess of syllables was assigned to me at birth."

He was confused by his choice of words — and by how each new word seemed to drag out to justify the last. He had found himself on the road because of his name — the first name he could remember having, whatever it had been. There was a horrible act tied to it now. He resisted telling anyone as he sat still — thinking about it was painful enough without speaking of the shame.

He left his first name behind after they threw him into a dark room. He escaped and renounced the name under the skies of the early morning. He left his home and everything that he had once known for what he did. When he left, he remembered what had happened — now the details faded with every step until all that remained were feelings of anger and shame. But he had left his name behind because that was the price of escaping.

He slammed his cup onto the table and thanked the saloon keep for his hospitality — people were much kinder on the road, especially in hamlets where people were used to errant wanderers passing by morosely. Felix stood up and left without making eye contact with anyone else in the bar. Keeping his destination in mind proved difficult — it kept slipping away even as Felix fought to keep it. He wondered if, like his name, the final place of his wandering would move away from him. He couldn't be sure that it hadn't already.

Before he left, he noticed a last sip of water in his cup. He hurried outside and offered it to the man in rags who drank it with a weak smile.

"Thank you, my friend," the man said.

Felix said nothing. He took the cup back to the bartender and stood in silence over the counter. Somehow the water was easier to give than the money.

"You're wasting your time with that beggar outside," The bartender said. "He's always there.

He just sits around day after day. A lot of would-be patrons and visitors come by here, see him and think we're all poor. We aren't all poor. Not here. It's a small town, but we get by, and by sitting right out in front there like that, he insults all of us who work for what we've got. Even if you want to help him, there is nothing a little water will do to get him off that bit of dirt. He'll still be sitting there tomorrow."

"I know," Felix said, unable to find the words to explain himself.

Confused, the bartender turned away and waited for Felix to leave.

It was as though his shame were the only thing that truly existed beyond the unspoken need to keep walking — to keep living. Everything else was an illusion that faded into the distance as soon as he left it — and yet, he gave the man a drink of water for reasons that were beyond him.

As he turned toward the road once more, he saw a man glaring at him from the other side of the town. Felix couldn't recognize the man — his scowling face carried a certain distant familiarity — but knew immediately that he was to be avoided. The man's eyes shone a hateful blue glimmer — seemingly glowing in the clear daylight sun. He grinned with teeth that were perfectly straight and blindingly white, yet his smile was crooked and sinister with an unspoken malice. He was large enough that he towered over each of the passing townspeople around him, but his size had no noticeable impact on his quick speed.

As soon as he felt his eyes, Felix hurried his pace and left the man behind — when he looked over his shoulder, he saw the man walking in his direction and increasing his speed with every step. He walked faster as he left the hamlet. Every time he looked over his shoulder, the man was following a few paces behind him.

"Stop," the man called. "I need to speak with you."

"I can't help you," Felix briskly responded. "I'm sorry."

The man was undeterred by the reply — it only seemed to annoy him. Felix began to panic — he was too tired to fight and there was nowhere to run, even if he had the strength to break into a sprint. He kept hearing the man's footsteps scraping the dirt behind him until they stopped near the entrance.

"Get off me!" The man shouted, his voice echoing into the air.

Felix turned to see the dying man gripping the man with the loud voice by the boot with an impossibly tight grip. The man with the loud voice struck the dying man's hand with his free boot and continued to shout. The dying man looked up and smiled at Felix.

The man with the loud voice broke free from the grip of the man in tatters only to stumble forward, nearly falling to the ground. Felix turned once more to the horizon and kept walking.

"Hey!" he heard the man in tatters cry, "This guy says he wants to buy the town!"

A ruckus sounded in the hamlet behind Felix as people clamoured toward the emerging scene.

After several paces, there were still no footsteps behind him — he turned and found nothing but the hamlet looking small so far in the distance. The man with the loud voice had disappeared.

He kept walking until a shape formed in his peripheral vision. The man in tatters emerged on foot, and glanced toward Felix as he walked.

"Could say we're even now," he said. "But I can't stay in that town now. Everyone will know that I lied soon enough. What's your name, anyway?"

"Felix." He replied without thinking.

"Good to meet you, young man. My name is Cuthbert Kahmekwaskawew." Felix stood still and turned to the man.

"I can't look after you," he replied sadly. "That drink of water was everything I could do for you."

"I'm not asking for your help." The man replied with a grin. "I don't need it — but still, I appreciate that drink of water. I was thirsty. But you don't look like you have any idea how to keep yourself walking. You sure you aren't lost? What are you, a prince or something? You must have riches if you can help a poor little man like me."

"Don't mock me, beggar," Felix snapped suddenly, stopping to turn and face the man.

"Beggar?" The man repeated, scratching the dirt from his cheek as his grin faded. "So, you're familiar with their ways. You can't have been on the road too long. I've also learned how they speak — I can trap you in a word. Your word is wanderer, vagrant, vagabond, tramp. What you do becomes who you are. You see me here with nothing, and you call me a beggar to feel above it all — but tell me, vagrant, in their eyes, what are you but a beggar who walks?"

Felix said nothing, turning back to the road. The man clasped his hand and stuffed some greens into his grip. Felix looked down to see a variety of wild herbs.

"You'll need those." The man in tatters explained. "These grow abundantly along the plains as long as you eat only what you need."

Felix smiled, but he stayed silent, pocketing the herbs. He nodded, then turned away, leaving Cuthbert in the distance as he ran from the commotion in the hamlet, blindly disappearing into the distant flats ahead.

TO REST DEEP IN LOAM

FELIX GLANCED OVER HIS SHOULDER several times as he ran into the horizon — even with the man gone, he kept imagining him reappearing. He ran until his breath gave out. He doubled over, his stomach turning.

When he looked up, he saw two figures by the side of the road — Douthcress sighed, turning his neck an old woman hunched over the motionless body of a young man. Felix looked around, hoping to avoid the sombre sight, but saw no other direction to go.

He gritted his teeth and tried to avert his vision, but his curiosity got the best of him — the young man's face had been so brutalized that he was entirely unrecognizable, and the tears of the old woman fell onto his stiff hands.

"His name was John-Norbert," the old woman said. "Remember his name. He was Norbert. John-Norbert Zace. He loved to make things. He made so many things when he could find wood. He loved that."

The old woman limply clasped Felix's ankle.

"Please remember. Please. Please remember this young man for his mother. Please." Felix felt his heart pound as he nodded slowly.

"I will," he said, unsure if he could keep the promise even as he made it. "I'll remember."

The old woman began crying as she thanked Felix. When she released him, Felix continued his journey to nowhere as she shouted his praises into the distance — but the strange, sinking feeling in his gut echoed louder in his mind.

The faceless heap that had once been a man — walking, living and speaking as Felix did — stung in his mind. Felix couldn't recall if he had ever seen a human reduced to such a state. As he walked, he tried to imagine what the corpse — what John-Norbert Zace — would have looked like, whittling wood for his mother on the side of the road.

It felt like he was keeping his word that way.

FOREVER JOURNEY

FELIX CONTINUED DOWN THE ROAD and watched as the sparse clouds drifted above him, powerless against the relentless clarity of the open blue skies. The sun beat down on his back and he felt himself stumbling to combat its heat. As the back of his shirt peeled from his skin, he realized he had been drenched in sweat.

As he walked, the image of the dead young man — of John-Norbert — stung his thoughts with every few steps.

He looked up, wiping his eyes as a smokestack emerged from the horizon. He blinked and wandered in its direction. As he approached, he heard voices join the sounds of the cicadas and the billowing wheat.

"It's some far-off place — that's what the paper was saying. The king fled somewhere else apparently. Such a coward."

"Did he? Yeah, I can't blame him. I'd probably do the same, were I in his situation. Wonder what the emperor wants with such a wasteland. There was nothing left when the soldiers were through with it."

"I guess territory is territory."

As the conversing voices grew louder, the stench of burning leather filled his nostrils. He fell onto a tree as his gut contorted with nauseous tension. He looked up before him and stared in disbelief as a pair of soldiers dressed in clearly marked empire uniforms — the red insignias highlighted against the green wool of their uniforms in the heat — standing over a pit of corpses before a hamlet of burning houses in the distance. The taller of the two men smoked a cigarette as he dug deep into the earth while his shorter colleague tossed a few more bodies into the pit.

"Hey!" The shorter man called, reaching for his rifle. "You there, stop!"

As he realized he had been spotted, Felix put his hands above his head and dropped to the ground, the motion coming naturally to his limbs. The taller man leapt over the walls of the pit and kicked his rifle into his hands, joining the shorter man as they approached Felix.

"Nice and easy now," the shorter man said. "Just stay still, answer our questions and don't do anything dumb. You understand?"

Felix nodded, his eyes turning to the pit of corpses — the stench was overwhelming. At a glance, he counted at least fifteen in the mass grave. He turned to the shorter soldier, keeping his eyes focused on the man's nose to avoid looking him in the eye. He made out their names, sewn to their uniforms with fraying thread — the taller man was Hunthridge and the shorter was Douthcress — but tried not to stare at them for too long.

Judging by the state of the thread, they had tried and failed to remove their names from their clothes.

"Good," the soldier said, softly levelling his gun. "State your name and your business."

"Felix Cabil Babimoosay." He gave himself a middle name on a whim, gulping down the terror building in his chest as his eyes fluttered toward the soldier's gun. He had chosen the name to add an air of dignity to himself. "I'm just walking — sir," he said, stuttering the additional word when the soldier — Douthcress — narrowed his eyes in disapproval.

"I'm derelict, sir," Felix said through a pounding heart. "I have no destination."

"You don't know where you're going?"

With a sigh and a sinking feeling, Felix shook his head. He looked to the ground to hide his tears as he felt the gun nearing his face.

"Do you know where you are?"

"I have no idea, sir."

"So," Douthcress sighed; he turned his neck toward Hunthridge but kept his gun pointed at Felix. "He doesn't know where he's going, he doesn't know where he is, and all he has is a name. Tony, what do you think?"

After a silence, Hunthridge approached. He looked first to Felix and then back toward Douthcress.

"Suits us fine." Hunthridge said.

"No, it doesn't. We don't know who this is."

"Look at him, Mike," Hunthridge snapped, his tone slowly growing nonchalant. "He doesn't even know who he is, and he doesn't know who we are. He has no idea what he saw, let alone where he is. He can't say anything to anyone."

Hunthridge turned to Felix with a raised eyebrow. "Isn't that right?"

"Yes, sir," Felix said, trying to keep his tone steady. "I don't know who you are, and I have no idea where I am."

Felix glanced around — the faces of the soldiers didn't seem satisfied. "I'm stupid, sir," he added hastily in the hope he sounded convincing.

Douthcress laughed, turning to Hunthridge. When Hunthridge smiled too, Douthcress lowered his gun and patted Felix's shoulder before standing him to his feet.

"It's best if you just forgot this whole thing," he said. "Just a bad dream, nothing more."

Felix nodded and when they told him to keep going and to keep slow, he took half paces until the men were out of sight.

* * *

He turned to see the remnants of a few more houses — the crumbling walls were covered in blood and ash. Felix tried not to stare but the stench that hovered above the roofs of the battered buildings was unbearable.

Two more shapes emerged beside one of the charred houses — more soldiers, each with the same uniforms as Douthcress and Hunthridge, their names just as legible despite the same failed attempts to tear the thread from the fabric. One — Umberden — sat, staring into the distance as another — Mackley — paced back and forth, emphasizing his words with his hands as Felix walked by.

"What do we have to feel guilty about?" Mackley spat. "Nothing! They do this all the time. McKay said himself we haven't killed enough of these traitors. This is our chance — we can prove to them that we can serve the empire as well as anyone else. We can prove to them that all the times they put us down — all the times they called us names, all the times they beat us and told us we were less than human and had the gall to insult our loyalty to the legion — they were wrong. Because of us, now the traitor will fear the barbarian as he did the men from the empire. Don't you waste another tear on them, Kyle."

"We aren't barbarians," Umberden said. "We found civilization."

"Sure, but civilization named us. That's what matters. That's who we answer to."

"We killed him," Umberden said, his eyes fixed on the ground. "We tortured him to death. That was us, Clayton. We did that."

"We did what they wanted us to."

The men fell silent as Felix walked by. They looked at him with blank expressions — they were nonchalant as though looking into a mirror. Felix stopped for a moment, looking into Mackley's hands — in his fingers he held a pile of photographs. Though Felix was too far away to make out the details of the images, he made out the likenesses of Mackley and Umberden and a blurred, red shape behind them.

Felix met their eyes — they were filled with terror and with guilt — and he turned away. He couldn't allow himself time to think about what he had heard. His mind was occupied with leaving as soon as possible.

But their words seemed distantly familiar in a way that confused Felix as much as it frightened him.

He shook his head as he walked through the remainder of the town, stopping only as he found another soldier, an officer, sitting on the outskirts, swaying back and forth with a bottle of whisky in his fingers. Through alcohol stains, Felix made out a name so far away he had to squint — McKay — on his uniform. A blood-stained axe was propped up behind him.

"I said don't kill him," McKay mumbled to himself. "I said do whatever you want but just don't kill him. He was going to give us something useful. Kill the rest. Don't kill him. Do whatever you want but don't kill him. I don't care just don't kill him. I said that. Traitors. All of them were traitors. Can't get away with that. But don't kill this one. Do whatever you want. I don't care. Just don't kill him. But no one ever listens to Mark-Adam. No one ever listens."

His eyes shot up at Felix as he lunged forward, stumbling over himself and falling on the ground, landing in a heap next to Felix's foot.

"Keep walking," the officer shouted into the sky, staining his uniform with grass as he writhed and struggled. "Keep walking — I'll take your head off. I'll take it off and stick you on a stake. Quit staring. That staring will be the last you do."

His ramblings echoed far into the horizon.

* * *

Felix slowly felt his heart stop pounding in his chest. When he was calm again, he felt the herbs from Cuthbert in his hand. He ate a blade of the grass and all the residual nausea faded.

He sighed and regained his breath as a caw sounded from above. A crow drifted toward the ground and hovered before Felix's face, keeping itself in the air with deliberate, rhythmic flaps from its wings.

"Where are you going, anyway?" The crow asked suddenly.

Felix walked in silence a little longer, and he let the crow follow — half of his mind pondered a reply and the other half was hoping the unanswered question would disappear into the air. He wondered still if he had lost his mind somewhere along the road, but when the crow continued to follow him, he felt compelled to respond.

"Forward," Felix eventually replied plainly, the word being the only thing that sounded accurate.

"Well, yes. But where do you want to end up?"

Felix felt himself growing annoyed. He kept silent and tried to pay no mind to the crow even as the question lingered in the air.

"It's fine if you don't know." The crow eventually continued a few minutes later. "Some people actually prefer to have no destination, but if this is a forever journey, you really should sit down soon."

"Why?"

"You're sweating a lot, Felix. If you aren't careful, you might get heat exhaustion."

"I'll stop when I need to stop."

"You mean you just walk until you can't anymore? You should really think about saving your strength, especially if you don't even know where you're going — let alone how long it would take to get there."

Felix could only let out a grunt in response.

After a few more steps, the crow stopped suddenly and landed on the ground. Felix felt his legs grow weak, and reluctantly he sat on the ground.

"Much better, isn't it?" The crow said. Felix slowly nodded.

"Now make sure to pick some more of those herbs. They last a while, but they won't keep forever."

Felix studied the herbs in his hand and matched them with the surrounding plants with a soft glance as the crow began to fly once more.

"Those men spared you for reasons you don't know and don't need to know — pondering their actions is a waste of energy. But remember, your stomach is much more predictable. If you don't eat often and well, you will die — it's as simple as that. Luckily, that's what these herbs are for. They've been eaten on this earth since time immemorial."

Without another word, the crow flew away. Felix sat in silence, his feet still numb. He caught his breath and turned over to one side, trying to sleep.

It was always hard to rest on the soil — the ground was rough and when it grew soft, Felix could feel the earth slowly turning as he lay on it. Sleeping never got easier. His rests were always dreamless.

When he awoke, his feet were still numb — only now two shapes emerged on the horizon.

Felix rubbed his eyes to find Umberden and Mackley approaching him.

DUST WALK

FELIX JUMPED TO HIS FEET only to fall onto his side after his toes proved too numb to carry him.

He stumbled on the ground, slowly crawling forward as the soldiers came closer. "Stop!" Cried Macklay — a gun clicking after his voice. "Stay where you are."

Felix froze, dropping his arms at his sides to show that his hands were empty. Two pairs of leather boots flanked him and four hands pushed him to his knees, as a rifle came into his face once more — only this time it was pressed against his cheek.

"Why'd Hunthridge and Doutchcress just let you walk?" Umberden asked suddenly. Felix shook his head. "Did you pay them off? Why?"

"I don't know," he sputtered. "I don't. I swear. I don't know. They just said I could go and I went. That's all. I didn't see anything. I don't know who you are or where we are. Nothing."

Felix felt his eyes grow with terror — after escaping the muzzle of a gun, he was there yet again. He thought briefly about looking away, but kept his neck stiff and still for fear that any sudden motion would startle the soldier and leave him dead on the plains.

"My name is Tyro Kyle Levy Umberden," Umberden said suddenly. "And to my right is my commanding officer, Optio Clayton Ephraim Mackley. We are currently situated just outside the town of Liditz Meadow — that's what it used to be at least. We just neutralized that town of conspiring degenerates under direct orders from the emperor himself."

With a crooked grin, Mackley nodded.

"That means you can kill him now," he said. "In fact, you have to."

"Wait! Wait!" Felix pleaded, throwing his hand up. "I can help you. I can help you. I know where the nearest town is."

"You think we don't know that?"

"I saw you — I've been wandering around long enough that I know what aimless pacing looks like. You're running low on food, aren't you?" Felix pleaded, hoping his bluff would be accurate by some stroke of luck. "I know these plains. I can take you to a hamlet. It's loyal to the empire. They can feed you there."

"Who's to say we didn't come from there already? Who's to say we need you?"

Felix heard a slight change in the soldier's tone. He forced a grin and feigned confidence to hide his pounding heartbeat.

"All your friends are weary," he said. "It seems you lost your map. And you can't wander off together — not if you want to hide what happened back there."

With a reluctant nod, Mackley gestured for Umberden to lower his rifle.

"You give us one reason to think you're up to something," Mackley said, looming over Felix and sending flecks of spit onto his cheek.

Felix nodded and stood to his feet.

"Take us to this town, get us some food and water and take us back here. We can't be long either. This is just a short walk."

"We're going west," he said, finding confidence in his voice with a glance toward the guns they carried.

He turned to where he thought a hamlet had been and started walking, hoping to find it within three days and that it would be friendly to the empire as he had said.

* * *

The three men walked for several hours in silence. Though he was never fully calm, Felix felt his nerves easing enough that he could think. He looked at Mackley and Umberden — both men were tired and wary, apparently having gone some time without eating anything substantial.

By the time he realized that he didn't know where they were going, he immediately began plotting to eat herbs from the ground and keep walking until either a hamlet emerged or the soldiers starved to death. Whenever their backs were turned, Felix plucked a few herbs from the ground as the crow had instructed and ate them quickly and out of sight. As they walked, Felix kept counting their bullets in his head from the little he could assume from the size of the rifles, hoping that they would keep their composure — at least until he could be rid of them.

Mackley suddenly stopped as the hot afternoon sun beat down on the plains. "It's getting too late to continue. We should make camp."

Felix shrugged.

"It'll prolong the journey," he explained. "Can everyone else hold out that long?"

"Don't question me. You don't get an opinion. Umberden, chain up this wild man so he doesn't run away — or eat us in the middle of the night for that matter."

Umberden nodded and took out a set of shackles from the green bag on his back, only for the sweat on his brow to grow deeper as he searched for something to fasten them to. He sighed and fastened them around Felix's ankles.

"If you run," he said, locking the chains. "At least you'll look funny before you die."

Mackley handed Umberden a hammer and a set of nails. With a nod, Umberden tapped the nails into the earth through the links in the chain, pinning Felix in place. Felix sat still on the ground as the soldiers prepared their sleeping mats and went to sleep.

*　*　*

As the night faded into the sky, Felix once again drifted in and out of sleep. In his seated position — a non-negotiable resting place with the shackles nailed to the ground under him — he could only lay his head on his shoulder and hope that he would relax long enough to fall asleep. The few moments of quiet rest he had were some of the worst he could recall.

The sudden sound of a flutter shook away the sleep from Felix's head.

He turned, trying to find the source of the noise, until a crow came into view. Felix gritted his teeth, annoyed at the abrupt entrance of the animal.

"How long have you been following me, then?" He seethed.

"I haven't been," the crow said, cawing with laughter. "Word has been going around about something really funny around here — you don't disappoint."

"I didn't see anyone."

"Well, it's not impossible to hide on a flat plain — difficult but not impossible." Felix looked at the ground and the crow hopped closer to him.

"You might be able to outlast them," she said, suddenly growing stern. "But they might just start getting even more unpredictable. Either way, you probably won't survive."

Felix sighed.

"It's not like I have a choice," he said with a grunt of pain from the tight shackles. "I don't know where I'm going. I can't fight them. I can't run from them. I can only wait them out and hope."

"I wish you luck, Felix Cabil Babimoosay," the crow replied, slowly drifting away and disappearing into the night.

With a sigh, Felix rested his head on his shoulder and tried to catch a few more minutes of sleep before the sun came up.

BURROW

IN THE MORNING, THE SOLDIERS JOSTLED FELIX awake. Umberden pulled the nails from the ground and started to remove the shackles but Mackley shook his head and turned back to the road. Felix stood to his feet and tried to walk normally, only to stumble under the foreign constraint of the chains around his ankles.

They prodded him along the road, irritated both when he walked too quickly and when he was too slow — occasionally even when his pace remained consistent. Eventually, Felix grew accustomed to the occasional nudge from the butt of Mackley's rifle.

As they went, the soldiers began conversing — their tone grew casual and they spoke as though they were walking alone, or at least out of earshot.

"Do you think this guy was involved?"

"No reason to suspect he was."

"But he could have been. Who knows why he was in Liditz Meadow? He might be able to tell us what we need to know. This could just save our skin. We might not need to report any failure to the emperor. We might be able to get away with reporting this mission as accomplished."

"We can do that anyway. We can say the responsible person was among the dead in that village. That's why we went there in the first place."

"He could still verify that, if he's involved that is. Do you really want to report a success only for us to get court marshalled when our failure unravels?"

"He could just as easily lead us up the garden path. I know you're eager to kill him — I am too — I've been itching for it since we picked him up. There's no sense in letting him live as soon as we get the supplies we need."

"Shouldn't we try to get some useful information out of him first?"

"You're forgetting your place, Umberden. I'm your commanding officer out here in the wilds. You don't get an opinion. When I tell you to do something, you do it without hesitation. Is that understood?"

"Yes, sir."

Felix stopped walking for a moment. Mackley jabbed him with the butt of his rifle. "Why did you stop? Did we say you could stop?"

"You're going to kill me?" Felix shouted. "Even if I show you to this hamlet, you will still kill me?"

Mackley chuckled. "We might, we might not. It's not really up to you what we decide, is it?" He scoffed, pushing Felix along with his gun and walking further. "I could be talking about you or maybe someone else. Either way, you don't get to decide if we shoot you or if we let you live."

Felix felt his heart pound faster. He had suspected the intent of the soldiers, but hearing it made it impossible to ignore or deny. With his eyes on the ground, Felix kept walking.

As he went, he heard the breathing from the soldiers growing strained. Their steps were unbalanced. When they nudged him along, their strikes grew slightly weaker and they started to wheeze. Felix sighed with relief as he went — the soldiers were beginning to starve.

* * *

Felix stared into the bright blue of the open sky — he was too tired to dread the worst any longer. Aside from a small hope that the slowing pace of the soldiers would finally stop as they inevitably succumbed to the elements, his thoughts were silent. Before, he was hoping a town would appear on the horizon, but now he was hoping against seeing anything other than the dry, desolate plains.

The silence in Felix's thoughts was broken as Mackley suddenly fell to the ground with a thud.

Umberden stopped and looked over his fallen superior. Felix took his eyes from the sky and turned to the ground. Mackley's foot was lodged deep in a burrow, contorting his leg into an unnatural bend. His head was draped over a rock and the tall grass was broken around his motionless body.

Umberden felt desperately for a pulse as Felix knelt down to see Mackley's face — his eyes were open wide and lifeless.

"He's dead," Felix said, the words coming with his realization.

Umberden stood to his feet and brandished his rifle, pointing it to Felix's head. Where there had been fear in Felix's chest, now he found only indifference as he faced the soldier.

"What did you do?" Umberden spluttered, the rifle shaking in his hands.

"He tripped," Felix explained. "We were walking and he stepped into that burrow and he tripped. I didn't do anything. It was an accident."

"You're lying. This is some kind of trick. We warned you. We warned you about what would happen if you pulled anything."

"What possible reason could I have for killing him and letting you live?" Felix sighed. "If you shoot me now, you're never going to find any water. You would only be joining me in death."

Umberden said nothing, lowering his rifle and picking up Mackley's weapon. He continued walking and Felix followed him, leaving Mackley where he had fallen. As they wandered forward, Umberden no longer nudged Felix with his rifle. He stayed silent with anger and fear in his eyes. His hands shook and his eyes shifted constantly.

Felix ignored the agitated soldier, the shackles knocking against his ankles.

LIDITZ MEADOW

UMBERDEN STOPPED ABRUPTLY in the middle of a field.

"This is our last stop," he said. "Tomorrow we go to the water."

Felix nodded, allowing the soldier's tone of forced confidence to slip through the air without comment — the argument wasn't worth being shot. He sat down and watched as Umberden hammered more nails into the ground to pin the shackles into place once more. The sky was already starting to go dark — the sun seemed to be setting earlier than before. He turned away and rolled out a mat to sleep on. Then, despite the hot air, he started rubbing his shoulders furiously for warmth.

Felix felt his stomach growling — he reached for a herb and started to eat it, only to drop the blade of grass as Umberden turned.

"You people disgust me," the soldier said, standing over Felix and blowing into his hands to keep warm. "You'll just eat anything off the ground. It's revolting. Now you understand this — I am not like you and neither was Clayton. We're civilized. Do you even know about tables and plates? Have you ever eaten a proper cooked meal in your life?"

Felix looked to the ground, hoping Umberden's shivering would cut his ramble short.

"What were you doing in that village?" Felix asked suddenly — the implications of the question escaped his mind faster than he could consider. Umberden glared back. "You might as well tell me. There's no one for me to tell — and you're just going to kill me anyway."

"I haven't made up my mind yet. For all you know, I might kill you in a few seconds or first thing tomorrow or five years from now when you've crawled into whatever mud hut you crawled out of."

"You seemed fairly certain yesterday."

Umberden grabbed Felix by the front of his shirt. The soldier's teeth chattered in the silence. "Now listen to me," he said. "I did what I was ordered to do. I did my duty for the empire. You could never understand."

"The empire ordered you to massacre an entire village?"

"They ordered my platoon to liquidate an encampment of traitors."

Umberden released Felix and paced quietly, sitting on the ground with a blank expression. "After the emperor was shot," he began, his tone growing grim and emotionless. "The would-be assassin fled somewhere out here. There was word of him running off to that village — to Liditz Meadow. They'd stolen some horses so we went to investigate. On the way, we saw a young savage cutting wood. When we asked where to find the village, he fled and we pursued."

"And you killed him with an axe," Felix said, recalling the corpse of John-Norbert and the bloodied axe behind McKay. "I passed that mess on my way to the village — or what you'd left of it."

Felix felt himself continuing to push — hoping that as long as Umberden was talking, he wouldn't be able to shoot him.

"Well," Umberden said with a chuckle. "McKay hates it when people don't cooperate. You'd hate him when he gets mad, let me tell you."

Umberden chuckled again, his mouth contorting into a wolfish grin. "But the kid wasn't talking. All he had to do was talk."

Felix felt his stomach turn and his eyes narrow. "His name was John-Norbert Zace."

"Well who can be bothered with that?" Umberden said, his grin fading. "What do you care?"

Umberden started pacing back and forth, keeping one rifle slung across his shoulder and the other shaking in his agitated wrist.

"We found the town anyway. So tell me, why run? It was pointless. He ran because he was one of them. Maybe he tried to kill the emperor, did you ever think of that? They all harboured that bastard — whoever it was — and our orders were to kill them all. So, we did. We found one of them hiding in the toilet so we tried to keep that one alive and find out which was the killer but these pathetic people are so weak — he died after just a few hours."

Felix fell silent, looking to the ground.

"Think what you want," Umberden scoffed, sitting down a few metres away from Felix. "But me and Clayton did our duty. Again, how could you understand? You're a civilian — worse, you're a barbarian. We might have grown up like you, but we're nothing like you."

"What?"

"We were like you once — uncivilized too. But we learned. We've outgrown your antiquated ways. I know civilization and I won't be stuck in the past — I'll be a full-fledged man of the present. Not that you would know what that even means. Hell, you're probably pitying that little runt."

Felix suddenly shook his head in fear.

"I'm not," he said, shaking. "I swear to you I'm not."

"No? Then why'd you kill Clayton?"

Felix looked to the ground. "I didn't," he said. "He fell. It was an accident."

"Then why am I so cold? What are you doing to me? What kind of curse is this?"

"No curse. You're starving."

Umberden stood to his feet and immediately brandished his rifle, pointing its muzzle at Felix's head. Where there had been indifference, suddenly Felix felt fear again.

"The kid in the village said his name was Abucar Vasusena." He cocked his weapon and placed his finger over the trigger. "You know him? Is that why you're killing us with this witchcraft?"

"No."

"Speak up!"

"No — no, sir, I don't — "

"Don't what?"

"I don't know him, sir. I don't know who that is."

Umberden nodded, his head bobbing up and down violently as his grin reappeared. "Did you shoot the emperor?"

"No, no."

"You hate the empire? You hate freedom? Did you curse the emperor too?"

"No, sir. No I don't. I'm not a witch. You're just starving. You should eat some of these herbs. You'll feel better."

Laughing, Umberden lowered his rifle.

"No," he said, lying down with a grin as he placed the rifles at his feet. "I'd rather starve than eat like an animal."

SNOW AND SAND

THE GRASSES OF THE PLAINS BILLOWED in the wind as Felix kept walking with the shackles still knocking at his ankles. Before the plants had been mere fixtures of the landscape — benign and unimportant — now when he grew hungry, Felix knelt down and found more edible herbs, giving him the energy to continue. He only hoped he could keep hiding them from Umberden's prying eyes long enough to outlast him.

His mind soon followed the ease of his heart and he felt his feet moving steadily against the soil as he calmly fiddled with the greens in his hand. Occasionally, he closed his eyes and let the wind of the plains brush over him.

In those, moments, he was still walking alone.

He almost fell asleep on the road, though his feet kept walking, still restricted by the chains. Umberden struck his gut and Felix opened his eyes again, seeing a tree in the blue sky — his eyes followed its trunk to a shallow pond at its root.

Umberden nudged him forward and slowly, and they wandered closer to the water — had he been alone, Felix would have assumed it was a mirage.

The air grew cooler as they approached and Umberden laughed with glee.

"Who needs your fake hamlet now?" He laughed, rushing to the side of the pond and drinking the water out of his cupped hands.

Felix tried to go to the water himself, suddenly feeling his parched throat — but he tumbled forward, tripping over his shackles and landing in a heap near the edge of the pond. Umberden laughed again and strode back towards Felix facedown near the pond's edge.

* * *

"You were trying to lead me around, weren't you? Damn savage." Umberden leapt forward toward Felix. "I'm nothing like you. I hate you. Filthy bush barbarian."

He took the rifle from his back and stuck it onto Felix's head — though he couldn't see the soldier, Felix knew he was wearing that same wolfish grin.

The gun was pulled back — a shot resounded. Felix shuddered, then turned to see a hole in a nearby tree, leaves cascading to the ground, birds flying fast in every direction. The noise resounded in his chest he as rolled onto his side, his ears ringing from the discharge.

His senses dulled, and he made out the sound of several splashes that pounded after each other in the pond.

A figure stood over Umberden, shaking him violently to keep him still in the water and shoving him beneath the surface — once he was below, the figure held him and maintained a grip that was indifferent to his futile struggles until he stopped moving. The figure finally stood back as the lifeless body of the soldier bobbed to the surface.

The figure said a quiet prayer as Felix wiped his eyes, his ears only now recovering from the sound of the gunshot.

As the figure concluded the prayer, he emerged from the depths of the pond. Felix had to squint a few times before he recognized the man in front of him as Cuthbert.

Cuthbert pulled Umberden's corpse from the pond and set it away from the shore. He fished a key from the dead man's pocket and unlocked Felix's shackles — his ankles dripped with sweat and nearly burned in the sun despite the cool air near the pond. The two men sat in silence as the wind billowed overhead. Felix felt an urge to continue walking but his legs still had to rest from the pain in his ankles.

The wind changed direction and the blue of the skies above faded to white.

Felix stood to his feet, even as Cuthbert remained still — the heat of the plains faded to a thin frost as snow drifted onto the soil and the grasses. Across the flat landscape, everything was covered in a thin sheet of white. Felix slouched and wrapped his arms around his knees for warmth.

"You can never predict the seasons on these plains," Cuthbert said, slowly pacing around the pond and drifting in and out of view as his boots crunched the snow where he walked. "The land has a mind of its own."

As Felix gasped, he saw his breath fade into the air above him. His fingers grew stiff and the ground began to spin smoothly in the direction opposite to Cuthbert's pace.

"Like many things in this life, survival on the land is a matter of question and response," Cuthbert explained, continuing to pace. "If the land asks you the question of hunger, you respond by feeding yourself — if it asks you about cold, you respond by keeping yourself warm. As long as you respond in accordance with its question, you will survive. If you look hard enough, the answers can be found everywhere.

"If you are going to wander, the only thing you need is a strong head. You have to find your thoughts and avoid letting them scatter too far. You must never lose sight of who you are. If you find people, try to help them and they will help you. The moment we turn on one another is the moment we create danger. Some try to meet danger with danger for the promise of brief safety — but this is nonsense."

Felix felt his head spin as he grew cold.

"I don't follow you," he said, beginning to shiver.

"If I had robbed you in the town when you gave me that water, that would have solved nothing. It only would have placed me in further danger — people who are attacked see nothing but the threat before them and they will do anything to survive. Remember that the constant danger is death by starvation and by exposure — in people, you find potential friends. If this man had treated you as his friend, perhaps he would still be alive. It's a shame."

Felix shook his head. "No," he spat. "That man was part of a platoon of monsters — they massacred a village. They tortured a man to death and chopped another with an axe. I saw it. Disgusting people. I hope it hurt like hell when you drowned him."

"They lost themselves. They were trained to act like monsters until they weren't acting anymore. The act replaced the men. If I had allowed him to live, you would either have died — or if he had decided to spare you that bullet, he would have tried to make you more like him. Killing is always a tragedy, Felix. It's a tragedy even when it's necessary."

Felix clenched his jaw, unable to find the words to respond as his thoughts turned to Mackley — Felix didn't kill him, but he wanted him to die.

"They said they were trying to find someone who attacked the emperor," Felix said, turning to the dead soldier. "Did you do that?"

Cuthbert slowly approached Felix and sat beside him — remarkably, he seemed unbothered by the cold despite the tattered state of his clothes.

"What would I have to gain?" Cuthbert scoffed. "Even if I did try to kill His Venerable Excellency Emperor Leicester Johannes Crosigk von Pearson, his son or his grandson would just take his place. It would change nothing — and I don't have the capacity to mount the kind of revolt necessary to topple the family. There would be no point."

As Cuthbert spoke the full name of the emperor — a name Felix hadn't heard for some time on the road — his voice carried a tone of mockery. He felt the sides of his mouth curl into a smile as he realized that such a tone carried no consequences on the plains.

"How did you find me?" He asked after a silence, standing up.

"I didn't go out looking for you if that's what you think," Cuthbert explained. "But the plains are deceptive. They aren't very large at all in spite of how they appear. I just went looking for water and I found you here. Now, I'm afraid I must keep walking — as should you — but I'm sure we'll meet again, vagabond."

Felix nodded, thanking Cuthbert with his eyes as they continued walking in separate directions through the flat plains.

FLAMES OF TIME'S ARROW

DAYS FELT SHORTER ON THE FLAT PLAINS. The land with no season seemed to eat the hours of the day and shorten the duration of sunlight over the grasslands. Felix had only just started walking — at least it seemed that way to him — and already the sun was setting and darkness had engulfed his vision once more.

He kept walking as his eyes closed and his feet grew weak. He found himself on the ground, unable to move his tired limbs but still too panicked to sleep — when Felix tried to rest, he found his heart pounding in his chest at an excruciating pace. As he lay still, he realized that he had gone at least a few days without spotting edible plants or drinkable water — in a few more days, he would die on the flat plains. Perhaps Cuthbert would eventually find him or the crows and nuthatches would make use of his remains if they found him first. If the man with the loud voice found his body, he would let out a small jolt of disappointment as he returned empty-handed. Felix wanted to grin at this imagined end, knowing it would foil his chase, but he was too tired to emote.

With a sigh, Felix lay still on the grass with his arm blocking out his face until he felt a small writhing under his arm. Felix struggled to turn his head but could only remain still as the writhing grew to the remainder of his body and began to carry him away. He couldn't see anything apart from the dimly lit landscape that slowly passed his vision.

The writhing continued and a bright bonfire inched into view — the writhing faded from his body and Felix caught a glimpse of a few crawling shapes scurrying away as he lay before the fire.

Felix pulled himself closer to the fire, hoping to catch some of its warmth.

The flames burned, swallowing a few logs before a pair of hands emerged from the darkness to toss some more wood into the orange glow. As the embers rose into the air, the face of a bald man appeared in the darkness. The man was grinning but with a twinge of distant melancholy in his eyes. He looked down at Felix and leapt over the flames in a single bound to stand over him. He took Felix and raised him upright, propping him up on a nearby stack of supplies. The man then sat in front of Felix, scanning him with a cold glance.

"My name is John Wotan Clempner," the man barked, taking a pair of glasses from his pocket and fastening them onto his hairless head. "But I suppose that doesn't mean much out here. So, young man, I won't even ask your name since both of us will soon be swallowed by the cruel thrust of time's arrow. I hope you understand. It's not that I'm rude — I'm not rude. I am a man of rational and progressive education with a liberal knowledge of manners in polite society but I simply can't find in my reasoning a justification for asking a question whose answer yields nothing of use. Time is coming for us — its arrow is poised to destroy yet another civilization.

"Our great modern civilization is under threat.

"Really, when I gave you my name it was a waste of our fleeting time, but it will be over soon enough — and putting a name to my face costs but a few seconds, but oh, how precious these seconds are for every second trickles us ever closer to the end. I just hope that you understand that I can't in good conscience ask for your name in addition to mine when we have such little time left in our era. Please take no offence — we must, each of us, understand our place in the grand march of our great civilization."

As he spoke, John Wotan Clempner jumped around and threw

his arms into the air to emphasize his points. Felix wanted to say thank you, but that doesn't interest me, I really must be going — only to realize that his ability to speak was stolen. By some unknown force his throat had grown unbearably sore and the words never left his mouth.

Felix tried to stand up and leave the man to his rambling, but his legs were still numb and tired. Felix was forced to sit and listen. He gulped in his swollen throat as John Wotan Clempner continued to speak.

"This end time is nothing more than pitiable squalor — the golden ages are all over now and we have nothing but their worsening recession to our name. That is the march of history, I'm afraid — we've reached something of an end to our peak and now the only direction is down. It's been that way for the last five hundred years, at least.

"I'm sorry — I'm confusing you probably. Most people are bewildered when I speak to them about this sort of thing — too many among us still fear the inevitable, like the cave dwellers who wandered this earth thousands of years ago feared the arrival of agriculture. Of course we couldn't live like that forever — of course not — those societies couldn't last longer than a few thousand years before they inevitably became cultures and cultures have only a thousand years to enjoy as civilizations. No one can blame anyone for making that step — it's just what happens. A thousand years of thriving and then a thousand years of decline over and over again until we're finally extinct.

What we are seeing in our time is no different. We have tried to defy the will and the order of the universe by challenging this decline period with laudable ideals of free thought, of development, of reason, of property, of sovereignty, of individualism and of pride in the hopes of outlasting the thousand years of thriving that constitute a civilization as the peak of a culture. It's tragic but admirable, you see, because we will of course decline like everything else — in fact, we already are — but we tried to break the cycle and the world will be made worse by our departure."

Felix squirmed internally as he heard "we" leave John Wotan Clempner's mouth repeatedly. Despite his insistence, Felix felt excluded from the speech for reasons that appeared distant to him. As John Wotan Clempner caught his breath and prepared to speak again, Felix pushed himself to his knees.

"But can we save it? Can we defy the inevitable and defeat time's arrow? We have already proven ourselves to be the greatest civilization of the greatest culture in the history of the greatest species to walk on this planet. But can we … "

Felix finally felt his legs and stood up, walking in a shaky limp away from the bonfire and letting John Wotan Clempner's voice fade into the distance. When his feet regained their strength, Felix began to walk briskly and deliberately in the direction where his shadow had been. Felix's eyes adjusted to the dark and he finally saw the flat horizon of the plains — the night was cold and he began to shiver as he walked into the violet darkness.

As the bonfire faded behind him, Felix felt warmth on him again and a strange bevel glow blinded him. He wiped his eyes and looked up again to find another bonfire.

Confused, he stood over the flames and watched them crack against the wood. He looked around and found no trace of any life until a lone shape crawled into the light of the fire. Felix inched closer to get a better look and a caterpillar adjusted into view. A stiff hand reached down and plucked the caterpillar from the ground. A few footsteps sounded from behind him as a soldier ran out of the darkness, clasping Felix by the shirt with a pleading grip.

"Please," he begged in a raspy voice. His uniform read McKay even in the dark. "Please don't let him near me, please. Please don't let him take me. Not me. Please."

Confused, Felix shook his head and tapped his throat to indicate that he couldn't speak. McKay kept chattering in terror, oblivious to Felix's silence. A rustle sounded and McKay sprinted forward, knocking Felix to the ground. McKay stumbled, falling to his knees and screamed again in terror, crawling now, as more caterpillars emerged from the darkness, covering the soldier from head to toe. He disappeared into the dark as his pleas for mercy faded from earshot.

Felix turned to see what McKay was running from, wondering if there was a figure behind the rustling. When Felix looked where he had been crawling last, there was nothing but a heap of caterpillars. He examined the caterpillar he had picked up — rows of sharp, rotating teeth glinted in its mouth against the firelight as it squirmed. Felix stepped back as the sea of wriggling creatures coiled forward, eager to pick at what was left of the soldier. He looked down at a straggler from the ravenous wave. With a squint, he watched as it rolled on its back, trying to find ground with its barbed legs as its mouth dangled open, desperately hunting for anything to satiate its appetite.

Felix turned away, his heart pounding even as he towered over the caterpillar. He stomped down on the lone bug, its body crushing against the hard earth beneath. Believing the creature was dead, Felix searched the horizon for an escape from the darkness. He felt underfoot a squirming mass — the curled remains of the stomped-out caterpillar were being feasted on by ten more, sprouting from the ground. Horrified by the cannibalizing brethren, Felix stepped back. The caterpillars retreated to rejoin the clew, leaving nothing in their wake.

He tried to call for help, but his swollen throat stung as though a growing thorn were compelling him to remain silent.

"… outlast the force that destroyed every other culture on the planet?" John Wotan Clempner's voice asked, continuing on from where it had left off when Felix had walked away. "I don't know but I think that the world is better off if we try.

"Of course, nothing could be better than what came before at the peak of our existence, but we can attempt to save what we have left. That is my project, you see. I have created a great sanctuary in the middle of this dump — hopefully in time, it'll be enough to save us from time's arrow."

Felix turned away only to find the bonfire before him once more. Each time he moved his feet, the bonfire positioned itself to stand just before him. When John Wotan Clempner was nowhere to be seen, Felix simply gave up and sat down.

"That's the purpose of these miraculous creatures," he explained. "I need them to save everyone we hold so dear — they eat nutrients and release them for the benefit of my sanctuary and for my health. The more they eat, the more things grow and the better we all are in the end — the younger I feel. I'm saving the world by saving myself, young man. I want you to know this because soon you will be part of my glorious effort too. I thank you for your service."

Felix choked as the pain in his throat seared and a wriggling clump fell from his mouth. He looked down to see a cluster of caterpillars fall to the soil and flee.

"I'm sorry for what must be done. I hope you understand that if our great, miraculous civilization is allowed to defeat time's arrow — if the world is going to be saved and our great gifts to the world are to be preserved — then we must take the necessary precautions. I hope that when my work is done, I will be able to sit back and listen to the applause of a grateful universe. You don't know it yet, young man, but soon you will realize that we are at the peak of human history and that it is our responsibility to break the arrow of time and keep running into the sanctuary that I have built with these great creatures. Of course, not much can be said for their variants, sadly. Too much free will. Whoever thought of a selfless parasite? Ridiculous. I tried to make one of them a king once, but the offspring believed too much in their own myth — they started serving the people in deed as well as action. They misunderstood, and now that buffoon is underground — another bloody mess to clean up. This is what comes of power, young man. Give power to the selfless and decay follows close behind."

Felix felt his eyes rolling, and his jaw remained set shut against his will. As he listened to the man speak, he began to plead with his hands for him to stop speaking — to shout with desperate hand gestures to enunciate his wild begging. John Wotan Clempner never stopped speaking as he ignored Felix and acted as though he were giving a speech to a large crowd. Felix fell to his knees, defeated, as John Wotan Clempner's words echoed louder in his ears.

When at last the man took a breath, Felix looked up into the air, asking with his eyes if John Wotan Clempner had finally finished speaking. John Wotan Clempner stood over Felix with his eyes crossed — after a few seconds, he stepped back and disappeared into the shadows of the night.

Felix looked around and heard nothing but the crackling of the bonfire. A log snapped in the flames, sending sparks into the air.

With John Wotan Clempner gone, Felix easily found his footing against the orange glow and walked away. His throat alleviated in pressure. He walked a few paces only to find himself walking toward the bonfire once again. Felix looked up — the sun was beginning to rise. In frustration, Felix kicked dirt onto the fire. He fell onto his knees again and shouted into the skies, falling to his side as the sounds of anguish left his lungs. He lay there as the sun rose over the plains, wondering how he could escape the bizarre prison of the bonfire.

"There must be some way out of here," he said to himself glancing about, sitting by the embers of the closest firepit.

A caterpillar emerged from the ground and climbed toward him. Felix relaxed his limbs and prepared to be carried again — unsure if he felt disgusted or terrified by the idea, but he had no other option. The caterpillar soon became many and the army approached him. Felix tensed and then relaxed his limbs as they crawled onto his hands — only to squirm against his skin as they bit down on his flesh. Felix began swatting blindly at the caterpillars clinging to his skin with puny, invigorated jaws.

The insects, however, kept flooding out of the depths of the soil, relentless, appearing to have devoured anything that remained of McKay.

Felix pulled them off and threw them aside over and over again as more caterpillars came to take the place of their fallen companions. Their teeth pierced his skin, leaving circular marks of impact across his arms and ankles. Felix forced himself up, fearing he too would join McKay's fate, and ran from the dying bonfire — toward the dim light of early morning.

* * *

Felix caught his breath and sat down again. The bonfire was gone along with the caterpillars and any other trace of John Wotan Clempner. In their wake lay a barren field where the plains had once been. Where once there had been grasses and other thin greenery, now there lay nothing but dry, hardened, useless dirt. Felix looked around and saw that the field the caterpillars had created while John Wotan Clempner had given his lecture stretched as far as his eye could see.

Felix stood glumly in the field in silence. He cackled loudly, stopping only as an absurd noise sounded. He turned as a voice laughed wildly into the skies. Slowly, the laughter faded.

Felix regained his breath and reluctantly kept walking — there was nothing else to do.

MAN WITH THE LOUD VOICE

FELIX CONTINUED TO WALK INTO THE PLAINS as the sunlight boiled the cool morning into a blazing afternoon. As he glanced behind him, Felix saw a shape emerging on the horizon. The man with the loud voice from the small hamlet faded into view, his eyes glowing in the distance, and an imperial sword's hilt fastened to his belt.

"Who are you?" Felix shouted over his shoulder as he walked. "What do you want?"

The man said nothing, and his pace only seemed to increase. Felix turned back to the road and began to run. He still had no direction — only a sense of urgency that propelled him into the horizon. He ran, forcing himself into a speed that clasped his lungs with a tight grip. Felix felt the urge to slow himself, but he looked back to the road and found the man quickly gaining ground — without a bead of sweat on his head. Felix made his feet go faster still.

Felix rushed along the road for a slow cluster of moments, his pace faltering even as he tried to go faster. The man still followed behind, steadily marching toward his target. Felix's knees gave way and he collapsed on the side of the road. A stream of torrid vomit spewed from his stomach. He coughed and regained his breath amid the acerbic stench in his throat.

"You're a difficult man to find, Gussie," the man said in a loud, booming voice with a tone that shook in his gut under withheld laughter. He stood over Felix, wrenching him from the ground by the wrist. "At least, that's what they said. But now, you make this easy. Do you want to get caught, or are you just plain stupid?"

Felix remained silent — he was reserving what little strength he had left to squirm out of the man's iron grip. He considered briefly insisting that his name was Felix, but it seemed useless. The man felt Felix wriggling and tightened his clasp, letting out a bout of laughter that resounded from his chest. As the man laughed, his arm shook, dangling Felix from side to side.

Felix let his arms go loose as he realized that he may never leave. He imagined what he had done that had sent the man chasing him across such a great distance. Then, while he was in the man with the loud voice's grip, the frightening realization dawned on Felix — it wasn't a trick of the afternoon light; the man's eyes were glowing with a low, terrifying glare.

Felix prepared for the man to do as he wished, when he felt his grip loosen under the force of his wild laughter — after one more forceful jolt, Felix was free. His feet hit the ground, and he blindly ran forward once more.

The man with the loud voice growled in anger and barrelled after him. The adrenaline in Felix's gut overpowered his fatigue and confusion — he thought of nothing but escape until his mind wandered in its new desperation. He thought of how aimless his journey had been before — now he had new purpose in his step.

Felix felt his foot splash in shallow water. Ahead was a rapid stream. He knew the man had caught up to him by the sound of his heavy strides alone.

"What good is this going to do?" The man demanded in his loud voice. "You run, you hide and you claw for your freedom, but what good is it supposed to do? I'm always coming for you, Gussie!"

"Tell me what I've done," Felix pleaded, falling to his knees. "I can't even remember who I'm supposed to be. My name isn't Gussie! Whoever you are, you must have some reason to stalk me into this wasteland. Surely, you aren't just doing this for your own amusement!"

"In fairness, I can't say I wouldn't say the same thing if I were you. I would try to say I'd forgotten who I am. What you've done — " He paused and stared into the distance, slowing his stride toward Felix.

"Do you think I tried to kill the emperor?" Felix said. "I didn't. I wouldn't."

"No, but your crime is no less severe."

"Well, what have I done then? Surely, you can tell me at least."

"You won't admit your crime? Maybe you forgot. Maybe the guilt is too much for you to handle. It's hard to say."

"Then how do you know you have the right man?" Felix blurted out. "How do you know it's me you're looking for? I don't remember doing whatever this thing was and you expect to hear a denial from everyone you find. Wouldn't an innocent man deny the crime he was accused of?"

"Perhaps," the man responded, standing directly over Felix. "But then, who would confess apart from a madman, a great fool or a man who was both remorseful and guilty? Shall I continue searching forever for someone so insane, so stupid, or so repentant that they confess to me on the spot? Just how common do you suppose great fools and remorseful criminals are? You fit the description of the man I'm looking for — the man I remember — and if you were guilty, I would expect the same words to come out of your mouth. You look like the August Orosius from all the posters, so I have to assume it's you, even if it's not."

He kicked Felix down, then unstrapped a large bag from his back and turned it upside down, shaking two round shapes out of it. Felix turned away as the severed heads of Douthcress and Huntridge thudded against the hard ground — their mouths were open, and their eyes remained wide with shock, but he could recognize their faces all the same.

"My gut told me that you walked by there, and I accused those soldiers of helping you. They panicked and pled because they knew they had done something unspeakable. It doesn't matter if it was that kid they tortured, the man they chopped to death or if it was the poor job they did of burning and then burying those thirty corpses because they paid the price. They begged for their lives one by one. It didn't save them, of course. They ended up right in that shallow pit they were digging — save for their cowardly officer who fled into the horizon. The best part is that they were following orders and doing what the legion does when they find greedy little conspiring villages — the real crime was their incompetence. That stench was appalling. But it doesn't matter anymore. Now no one has to worry about the scandal that might follow if that news reaches the public. Those miserable excuses for officers will die in the plains and their secrets will die with them. That keeps the nobles sweet — it makes the people trust them more — and it means a nice bonus for me when I get back. You do a few more favours like that for me, and I might just let you keep running — if only it were up to me.

"That's what it takes to make justice — everyone is guilty of something, but it's so much bigger than matching crimes with punishment. Justice is an ideal, it's something for people to believe in so that they're safer and more docile."

Felix looked at the severed heads as blood pooled from the necks and stained the soil. He turned back to the man with the loud voice, feeling his attention growing weaker as his concentration moved to his words.

"You see, it really makes no difference whether you are playing games with me or not. The people of the Republic are angry and scared, and they need a face for the crime that was committed in broad daylight in their streets. The faster we can grant them this wish, the faster the crime will be considered answered, and they can get on with their lives. Not to mention, it damages the reputation of our great city — the centre of our dear Republic — to have a crime investigated for too long. It makes us look like amateurs — 'the legion of amateurs' isn't a useful image for our organization that we can afford to allow. How would you feel as a citizen of the wealthiest, most advanced civilization on the planet only to hear that the last line of defence between you and barbarism is a group of incompetent, bumbling morons who take several months to catch a single criminal? So we have to compensate for this wasted time by capturing yet more criminals — like these pathetic traitors to the empire. Do you understand what I'm saying, Gussie? I don't like lying or keeping things from people — you should at least know why I'm bringing you in.

"Even if you were innocent, arresting you would still be enough to satisfy my purposes — that is the price of order. You must understand this isn't anything personal. I'm just doing my job. If you come with me this time, I promise, you won't be put back in that dark cell — maybe I'll even bring you something good to eat when you behave yourself."

The man with the loud voice cleared his throat. He put a firm hand on Felix's shoulder and gave him a look of sympathy through his bright glowing eyes. Felix felt his eyes turn to the ground in defeat.

"I'm sorry, alright?" The man said, his quieted tone still booming through his loud voice. "Let's try and make this quick — that's better for both of us. You don't want to end up like your friends, do you?"

Felix wasted no time in brushing the man's hand from his shoulder before his grip could tighten. He stumbled back, then ran again, paying attention to little beyond the desperation of his dash, until another splash struck his foot, only for him to realize that the current of the stream was the only place to go. With a grin, Felix leapt into the water and let the current carry him downstream. The man with the loud voice stood still, a look of defeat creeping onto his face as he faded out of sight and his glowing eyes faded into the horizon.

* * *

After a short distance down the river, Felix let out a heavy laugh that carried in the sky as he drifted with the current.

As the water carried him, Felix felt the relief in his veins turn into a placid peace. He rested the tension in his limbs and let the stream push him gently along. It was difficult to remember to move his arms and keep himself afloat — if he sank too far below the surface, the current would soon become his enemy and drown him in the stream's shallow depths. As he gently pushed his body toward the surface, Felix watched the clouds moving by. The bright blue of the day sky soon turned to the deep velvet mauve of night.

With another breath, Felix ran his feet gently along the bottom of the stream to slow his pace, but the current kept pulling him just as quickly as before. He held up his feet once more, letting them rest on the surface of the water with his toes poking slightly out. He puffed his chest in and out of the water to keep himself afloat, but otherwise, he was perfectly still.

The sky moved over him as his thoughts turned to Umberden, Mackley and the other soldiers — he couldn't bring himself to feel sorry for their deaths but something burned in his mind as he recalled the image of each of their corpses — of Mackley laying lifeless in the grass, of Umberden floating limply in the pond, of McKay screaming in agony as the worms swept him into the darkness and left nothing behind, of Douthcress and Hunthridge's severed heads rolling on the ground with expressions frozen in terror. He shook his head and dismissed the thought, trying to keep himself from slipping under the surface.

As the moon rose into the sky, Felix gently turned his head to the side to watch the waters slowly move past him. He relaxed into the current and wondered how far the stream could carry him.

DOWNSTREAM

THE RIVER PUSHED FELIX ALONG until the sun rose again. He wasn't certain when he had slept — only that he must have since he didn't feel tired as the light of the sun swelled into the skies. He continued floating until a firm hand reached into the water, fished him out and dropped him onto the ground. When his eyes adjusted to the stillness of the soil, Felix saw an old woman with a sunspot on her forehead towering over him.

"You're lucky," she said. "A little further and you would have struck your head on some rocks. Tell me, what on earth were you doing in there anyway?"

Felix said nothing — his head's spinning made listening difficult enough without a reply. With a heavy sigh, the old woman sat down beside him and lit a fire from her tinderbox. When his head was finally still again, Felix stood up. The old woman glanced toward him but remained facing the fire.

"You must be travelling somewhere," she said. "People rarely come this way unless they are passing through. So tell me, young man, where are you going?"

"I don't know," Felix said. "Maybe I've forgotten, but I've just been walking forward. I just want to stay alive."

She turned to Felix and studied his expression. With a sigh, she turned away from him. "People are talking now," she continued. "From the chattering masses of the hamlets, I hear rumours of a tall forest in the middle of these flat plains. A forest shouldn't be here, and it doesn't belong, but it's here all the same. Some say it was planted by human hands and some say it sprouted out on its own but everyone can agree that there's a demon that lives in the woods — that's it's a place few people leave alive.

"Now, these people are mostly misled, you see. They think that the demon is a blessing to the land and the forest is the first sign of life," she reached into the dirt and extended her arm to Felix, showing a small pile of crawling ants in her hand. "But if they looked, they'd see that life is all around them, and really, this soil is all we need out here. This soil is disappearing more all the time, and so are we. Lies spread quickly — in fact, some of these liars are convinced that spreading lies to the four corners of the earth is their burden, their purpose. They lie so much that they think they're telling the truth. I wouldn't be surprised if this man chasing you were one of them."

"No," Felix replied suddenly. "This man is chasing me because of something I did — I know it. This is just what has to happen now. I can't blame him for hating me. That's all we little, pathetic creatures know how to do."

"Both things might be the case — he could be misled, and he could also be chasing you for something you did. Maybe he doesn't even know what it was, and you're just worth a lot of money to someone. How do you know he hates you anyway? He might not think about you at all beyond the money you'll bring him."

"We're all monsters — every single one of us," Felix felt his tongue rattling wildly against his teeth as he ignored the old woman's question. "Every human being is a stinking pile of greed and hate. You and I are no exception. We're all just waiting to kill each other. Since the dawn of time, we haven't done anything else — that's human nature for you. We created societies to stop us from murdering one another. All any of us can do is fight to survive in this mad world we've created."

"Then why did you help your friend in the hamlet? Is he

a monster?" Felix looked silently to the ground as the old woman rubbed her sunspot.

"I used to think as you do," the old woman sighed. "When I was younger, that was how I saw the world. I had yet to see. But then I realized something — it's the perfect excuse. If we truly are greedy, hateful, violent creatures by nature, then we have no reason to try to be anything else. I'm telling you now, it doesn't have to be that way. We were taught to act in that manner — like there is no other way of being in the world — and we have forgotten who we truly are. It is the easiest thing in the world to believe their fables about human nature and never be anything else. If you'd rather get out of the difficult work — the agonizing, unending task of changing and learning to be better, you can. This is the most frightening thing that people have to realize. We only have ourselves to blame — not some vague idea of what we're like deep down — because we let ourselves end up like this, and only we can decide what it means to be human with our own conscious thought. We've learned how to be careless and greedy and hateful, but we can learn how to be better too. No one ever said that undoing thousands of years of learning is an easy task. But we act outside of this false image of ourselves — just as you did in that hamlet. Even as you proclaim us all to be monsters, you refuse to act like one."

Felix shifted his face in the darkness, letting out a small hum from his mouth as he stepped back — it was the only reply he could muster. The old woman glanced toward him and edged nearer.

"I've been to the forest myself — I'm just returning from my second voyage through it," she continued, changing the subject. "I can tell you that if you go through those woods, you will find yourself again, and you will have a direction — endure slightly, and a better place awaits you just over the horizon. It's either that or you lose yourself wandering this land."

"Is there a difference between aimlessly following my shadow and aimlessly following my survival? Either way, it seems like I'll be wandering around these plains indefinitely."

"The difference is hope. You have to believe that there is a better place out there somewhere for you."

"And that won't drive me insane when I inevitably find nothing? I need food, and I need water, and I need shelter. How is hope going to keep me alive? Can it feed me? Can it put walls and a roof over my head?"

The old woman turned her face away from Felix.

"In the end," she said. "I suppose it's entirely your choice — you can take a chance on hope, or you can condemn yourself to aimless wandering. You know what wandering is, but you don't know a thing about hope — that much is clear — so how can you be sure of what hope can and cannot do?"

Felix sat in silence and turned his attention to the fire. The old woman was making a stew, tossing plants from the soil into the pot. She whistled to herself as the heat from the fire gently pushed toward Felix. He felt a chill trickle down his spine — the stream had made him cold, and he only now noticed the cool morning's wind.

He felt the water pour down his back and his arms as he sat back. The old woman remained focused on the stew, but her thoughts radiated from her as she stirred the pot. Felix looked out into the distance and let the heat slowly dry him as the stew came to a boil. The old woman took two bowls and filled them with the bubbling liquid. She passed one to Felix but told him to hold it still.

The old woman stared at him in silence as she sipped her stew. When the bowl in Felix's hands went lukewarm, he finally drank it. The old woman smiled and waited for him to finish eating before she took it. He sat still for a moment, thinking of where his wandering could take him.

Immediately, the thought exhausted him.

"Can you show me this forest?" He asked.

The old woman chuckled, the sunspot on her forehead bobbing up and down. She caught her breath and turned back to him with a look of bewildered amusement. Felix had to look away to hide the embarrassed expression that was forming on his face.

"No," she replied. "I should be getting back soon. I'd tell you to come with me, but you'd only get lost in the woods — the trees can confuse you if you're used to this flat horizon, and it will only make matters worse if I try to explain it to you. You have to find your own way. If you don't pass through them on your own, you'll just lose your way and get killed — you can meet me on the other side when the time is right. If you want to find it, all you have to do is follow your shadow. Keep going that way, and you'll find it in a few days' time."

Felix stood in quiet disappointment, but nodded himself into an acceptance of the old woman's reply. She stood up and wished him luck before she walked away and faded into the dark of the night. Felix lay his head against the soil and let himself drift away into a dreamless sleep.

When he awoke, Felix stood up and stretched his arms into the sky. Above, the plains were clear and blue as before — the wind swayed the trees behind him.

* * *

He walked slowly, following his shadow as the old woman had instructed. He didn't know how long the journey would be, but finally, he had a purpose. It made it feel much shorter than the directionless wandering of before.

A crow fluttered over his head as he walked.

"I overheard you talking last night with that old woman," said the bird. "And she's right, you know — you'll lose your mind out here like this. You don't have enough people for it to make sense. You're going to have to find something — somewhere."

Felix nodded, slowly. "Then I had better get going while we still have daylight."

He walked slowly, following his shadow as the old woman had instructed. The crow flew overhead, eagerly watching Felix's movements.

A short distance passed before Felix's mind again wandered. He stopped following his shadow and started following the stream instead.

"You moved away from your shadow," the bird said. "Any particular reason why?"

"It's this stream," Felix replied, slowly making sense of his decision as his stomach growled. "I'm bound to find somewhere to eat if I just follow the stream."

"If you're hungry, you've still got plenty of bittercress. Then there's some burdock, some hyssop."

"No, no. I need something real to eat. I need somewhere to sleep proper, and I need some walls. There's bound to be a town at the foot of this stream, and that is much more promising than some forest — assuming that forest even exists at all."

"That's not what the old woman instructed, Felix. You should listen to her."

"Who was she anyway? Just some crazy old woman from the plains? It sounds like a good way of getting me killed — I'm not having a repeat of that lunatic with the loud voice or of those crazed soldiers. I know where I want to be."

Felix continued down the stream. The waters bent around a group of trees, and a shadow formed before him as he passed. Felix's glance met the shadows, seeing the buildings with little shapes moving beneath them tucked behind the forestry in the far distance. Without a second thought, he hurried to the town.

PART II

GUIDED BY POLARIS

TOWNSHIP OF DOUFSANCTVILLE & AVARAMCK

FELIX WALKED FOR SEVERAL HOURS, his euphoria taking him into the night. He smiled and felt his steps growing faster as he wandered toward the distant lights of the town.

A welcome board's blurred shapes focused into letters: "Well come to The Township of Doufsanctville & Avaramck," the misspelled sign read. Felix stood for a moment, wondering if the sign to the town was only in his head — either way, Felix persisted.

He turned from the sign and then back to the road. A wagon emerged from the darkness and stopped near the outskirts of the town. Hesitantly, he approached. Felix tapped on the wood of the wagon and stood in silence as he awaited a reply.

"What do you want?" A dishevelled woman said, emerging from the wagon door.

"I'm a traveller. Do you know anywhere in town I could get some food for the night? I'm quite tired."

"You're not a traveller," The woman said, scanning Felix. "You're a fool. If you had any sense at all, you'd stay clear of this town."

"Why's that?" Felix asked, worry burrowing itself into his tone. "There's nothing out there for miles."

"Nothing is still better than this dump," The woman spat. "At least you won't be suddenly evicted from living in the middle of nowhere. Now get gone. I need to sleep."

The woman slammed the door shut, skimming Felix's nose. He swore, covering his nose with his hand from the pain.

He walked into the streets and looked about as busy faces ignored his gaze and hurried in directions unknown. Felix waded through the bustling crowd, quickly feeling out of place as people marched around him with irritated grumbles. Despite the late hour, everything in sight was in a stiff, static and unfeeling motion.

When the crowd passed by him, Felix was met by another irritated noise — a large dog, standing tall enough to bite at Felix's waist, barked and howled at him from across the street. The crowd dispersed, leaving the two men to face the guttural noise and it filled the air. The dog's frantic warnings were soon followed by a growling as it bore its teeth.

"She's a bullmastiff," A voice said, and a man came into view, holding the dog back with a leash. "She doesn't like you at all — I don't like you either. You look strange and useless to me but I can make her calm down if you give me five lire."

"I don't have any money," Felix said. "Don't be ridiculous."

"Well, then I guess you'd better get running — leave now, and I might call her back once you've reached the city limits."

The man prepared to drop the leash as the door to a store opened. An old man with a bristly, greying moustache emerged and stood with his hands on his hips. He reached into his pocket and took out a handful of money.

"For pity's sake, Dominic, you cheap bastard," the old man said. "Here's ten lire. Leave this kid alone and go back to sitting on welfare so the rest of us can work for a living."

"Welfare!" The man scoffed, yanking back his dog and swiping the money with his free hand. "I don't have any more welfare since you people cut it all. I'm out here keeping these bloody parasites out of Doufsie, but oh no, we owe it all to Gulliver Slack, the esteemed shopkeeper. You're a true pillar of the community, you are — twiddling your thumbs behind that counter all day."

"Don't push it, Dominic."

The man with the dog sneered and left, pulling his growling animal with him. Felix turned to the old man with gratitude in his eyes.

"Thank you," he said, but the old man held out a hand to stop him from talking.

"That's Dominic Holsapple," he explained in a grave tone. "He's our town guard — I just saved you from being another catch on his record. Would have been quite a night for him too — just finally evicted Mitto Welwood. Two catches in a single night — first he'd have made in seventeen years. Still, one is enough to make him celebrate at the bar and leave decent people alone."

Mr. Slack chuckled to himself, stopping as he scanned Felix more carefully.

"For the record," Mr. Slack continued. "As much of a dullard as Holsapple is, he's right for once — you don't look like the sort of person I'm inclined to trust. I reckon you're here and you're up to no good, but I'm a hardworking man and I could use a hand. You work for me, I'll pay you and I'll give you a place to sleep at night. If you want to be useful to the town, follow me to my shop. If you want to stay broke and useless, stay put."

* * *

He followed the old man into his store. Mr. Slack threw open the door to his store, leaving it to swing as Felix stepped through.

"I'm Gulliver to the customers, but to you, I'm either 'sir' or 'Mr. Slack,' depending on whether you're talking to me or about me. I run a tight ship around here — we get stock from the Republic and we sell it to anyone who comes through with enough money. You laze around, you don't get paid — end of story. First aisle's food, second aisle's non-perishable food and the third aisle's supplies — your fuels and wood and that sort of thing. If you have any questions, ask yourself if they're worth repeating before you come crying to me, understand?"

"Yes, sir," Felix responded immediately, granting him a slow nod from Mr. Slack.

"Good, then let me show you to your room." Mr. Slack took Felix to a small room under the stairs at the back of the store. It was small — a single bed with a straw mattress under a naked bulb — but Felix was in no position to complain.

"Rent's two thousand lire a month," Mr. Slack explained. "But since I'm just upstairs and you're working here anyway, I'll just take that from your weekly wages. The toilet's just at the back of the store — you're responsible for your own toilet paper — and if you need to eat something, there's a diner up the road where you can take fifteen minutes of lunch. Any longer than that and I'm taking it off your pay. I'm not paying for your meals — "

"Felix." Felix felt his heart sink as the man glared. "My name is Felix Cabil Babimoosay."

"Yeah," Mr. Slack replied, biting his lip with a sigh. "Never interrupt me again. Now get to the front of the store. We've got stock that needs to be put on the shelves so the store doesn't look broke. I expect you to be quick about it."

Mr. Slack bolted around and Felix followed him. Immediately, they found the boxes at the back of the store and unpacked their contents onto the shelves. A woman entered the store and asked about the new assistant with a tint of disdain in her voice — when she left, Mr. Slack scanned the shelves. He stood in silence until Felix stopped working.

"Listen," he said. "People around here don't really like strangers. Try to keep out of sight from the customers for the time being, alright? They'll get used to you after you've settled in a bit — then you won't be a stranger anymore. Just try to remember, they're sensitive. You just look a bit suspicious to them, you know? We have problems with outsiders all the time — don't take it personally."

"I'll try not to, sir," Felix replied, waiting until Mr. Slack had finished before speaking.

Mr. Slack nodded and went back to the counter. Felix returned to the boxes. When the door opened to announce another customer, Felix went to the back and stayed put until the customer left.

He went back and forth until the shop closed. Mr. Slack handed Felix a stack of money and dismissed him with a wave of his hand. Felix pocketed his earnings with a grin and stepped outside.

Felix found the diner closed. After wandering through the streets, he found a small bar and crept inside. He asked the bartender for some food in exchange for his money. The least expensive drink was still twenty lire. Felix found himself combing through the money in his pocket — Mr. Slack had given him a hundred lire — and after a glance at the menu, he realized that, at best, he would be leaving the bar with sixty-five. With a sigh, he ordered soup and a glass of beer — the cheapest options available.

As he sat, eating the soup, Holsapple appeared next to him.

"So you're staying then, are you, kid?" He said, his breath stinking with alcohol. "Well, I can always let Enza bite your legs off anytime I want. Every week I see you, I want five lire, or you'll be crawling out of Doufsie — and I could use a laugh, you know. Life's been boring these last few weeks."

Felix gritted his teeth and handed his money to the guard. With a grin, Holsapple pocketed it and slapped Felix on the back with a firm hand.

"I can see this working for everyone, kid," he said, slurring his speech. "You pay me, I hold Enza back, you keep your legs. Everyone wins. That's how we do things around here. Win-win … win-win … that's the Doufsie way … "

Holsapple trailed off and stared into the distance when he realized that Felix was no longer listening to him. Felix turned, smelling the alcohol on the man's breath — his glassy, bloodshot eyes darted toward Felix and he spoke once more.

"You must have come from somewhere — nobody just sprouts out of nowhere. Nobody, not even Gulliver — much as I hate to admit I'm from the same town as that freeloader — just sprouts out of thin air."

"I don't know," Felix replied. "I can't remember."

A silence fell over the two men as a band stood up to play. A woman from the band ran to each patron with a hat as the rest of the band stood at the front of the room, waiting in silence with their instruments. The woman approached Felix and shook the hat toward him.

"No one listens for free," Holsapple explained. "Just drop fifteen lire in the hat. These guys — they play good music. Maybe you got that for free back home, but here, you pay up."

"Yeah, yeah," Felix replied, tossing some money into the hat.

The woman disappeared and the sounds of a fluttery, mellow tune swelled in the air.

Holsapple turned to Felix and leaned forward. His eyes searched for Felix's glance.

"I have a right to know," he said, trying to shout over the sound of the music. "Now, tell me, where do you come from? I have a right to know. No more lies."

"The house," Felix replied, hoping his answer would satisfy Holsapple's curiosity. "I'm from the big farmhouse just out of town — gone now of course. That's why I left."

Holsapple burst into laughter until he coughed.

"You mean the farmhouse on the way into town? The only building for miles outside of the city? That house? That's the one you mean?"

Felix nodded.

"Some bleeding heart good for nothing had it and then he went bankrupt! The moron — he gave food away for free to anyone who asked, and then he couldn't pay the bank. Cried like a little girl too when he had to go back into the wilds. They took the house and left it there. That was years ago! That's from when my great-granddaddy was a town guard! It was old Jebediah Holsapple that chased that imbecile out of town. That's an old joke in Doufsie and you're telling me you've been living in that decrepit old house? All covered in weeds and sunken into the dirt? Maybe Gulliver buys that nonsense, but I don't — next time you lie, it'll cost you. I hope you enjoyed your last freebie."

Holsapple stood up and stumbled out of the bar as the music reached a crescendo. Felix sat, deciding what he would have to say when the guard asked the same question the next morning. When he couldn't find an answer that sounded convincing, he gulped down the last of his drink and darted away from Holsapple as he went back to the store.

Felix ignored the sounds of Mr. Slack's snoring from the upper levels as he walked through the empty store. He went to the back of the store and crept quietly into the little room under the stairs. It was small — barely large enough to contain the bed. Felix laid on his side, sleeping faster than he had in some time.

OPPIDAN DELIRIUM

A WARM DARKNESS SETTLED into the night. Several times throughout, Felix awoke for reasons that remained unknown to him. Though the straw mattress on the bed scratched at his back, it was preferable to the hard ground of the plains where he had become accustomed to sleeping. No wind blew over his face and there was no dirt against his neck. He slept well, but he could never sleep long. Each time he woke, the air was warm, and his head spun with confusion — nothing in the room could explain why his sleep was disrupted.

He could only turn his face to the side and try to sleep a little longer.

* * *

Felix was finally woken up by a tapping at his window. Rubbing his eyes, he peered out of the glass and saw a familiar figure looking back at him.

"Sorry," Cuthbert said, glancing around the small bedroom. "I hope I didn't disturb you. May I come in?"

Felix nodded, half-convinced he was still asleep. Cuthbert looked mostly as he had before — his clothes were still torn, and his hair was still a tangled mess that dangled from his head, but his boots were somehow in better shape.

"What are you doing here?" He asked, stepping aside and letting Cuthbert sneak inside.

"I've been here a little while," Cuthbert explained, closing the window behind him. "Just stopping by for a few days."

He sat on the floor and studied Felix for a moment.

"I thought I recognized you when you came into town. Strange that we keep running into each other like this."

Felix sat up, peering down at Cuthbert and wondering about the purpose of his sudden visit.

"I've lived in places like this before," Cuthbert explained. Felix fluttered awake again. "It's always the same. It never takes longer than a day."

"What are you talking about?"

"You can't rest because you think you should be working. If that boss of yours thinks you're lazy for even a second, you could lose everything. That's your worry, even if you don't know it yet."

"I'm just tired. I should rest. It's a busy day of work tomorrow."

Felix lay his head back on the scratchy straw pillow, trying to sleep again — hoping that Cuthbert would fade into the darkness like any other strange dream.

When he awoke, Cuthbert was still sitting on the floor — just as he had been earlier.

"An old woman I met in a small town once called it oppidan delirium — just some fancy words for what these roads and buildings do to you. These towns drain the life out of you until all that remains is a stumbling shell of a person. The town doesn't want you thinking or doing anything apart from work. The fog that pollutes and hollows your mind and kills your dreams — that's oppidan delirium."

"Are you finished? I'm trying to sleep."

"You just woke up again, Felix."

"Stop messing around. I have work tomorrow."

"I'm not. It's the town. It's oppidan delirium. It doesn't want you to do anything except work. It's poisoning your mind. That's what I keep trying to say."

"I'm not working now."

"Because you can't physically. You still feel like you should."

"No, Cuthbert. I know I have to rest. I could if you would just stop talking to me."

"Then why can't you stay asleep?"

Defiantly, Felix turned onto his stomach and shut his eyes firmly as the straw poked through the pillow case and jabbed at his cheek. He threw the blanket over his body and turned into the pillow. He sat in the velvet darkness until he stopped feeling the straw — only to wake up again. Felix lay still, gritting his teeth. He cleared his throat and sighed.

"I can hear you grumbling over there, Felix," Cuthbert continued, still unmoved. "You can't rest no matter what you do. It doesn't take long before the delirium takes hold of you. It's not going to let go — even when you get used to it, it just takes over."

"Why are you still talking to me? I can't sleep because you can't shut up."

"That's uncalled for, Felix. I didn't talk to you at all for the last hour — you still woke up three times."

"You yammering on can't be helping. What do you know anyway?" Felix snapped, standing to his feet. "When I found you, you were begging for scraps on the side of a dusty road. Now you're following me around like some kind of pathetic dog."

"I'm just trying to help, Felix."

"Well, maybe I don't need your help."

"If you don't want it, that's up to you," Cuthbert said, slowly standing and walking back to the window. "But you fell asleep again during that conversation — and now it's daybreak. Did you even notice?"

Felix scrambled out of bed — his vision was flooded by golden light as birds sang outside the window. He rubbed his eyes and stumbled about, finding his footing. Despite the short rests of sleep from the night before, he was still exhausted — his head was spinning, and he could only think of falling back onto the bed to sleep for a few more hours.

"You'd better hurry up now," Cuthbert said. "The last thing you want to do in a town like this is end up late. Here, there is nothing worse to be than lazy — and late and lazy are the same thing to them. You can work harder than anyone else has in the history of this town — if you're late, you'll still just be lazy. Just be glad you only have a hallway to walk down — the first time I tried living in a town, I had ten streets. You can sleep a little more than you would if you had to go across town."

"I'm so tired. I can barely stand."

"I know. It's an adjustment from living outside. Now, they have a clock and there are consequences when we don't keep to it."

Felix stood back, looking around at the walls around him. He put a hand against the drywall, trying to stand himself upright. As he ran his hand along the surface, a shiver climbed his arm despite the warm room.

"I don't miss the wind — or the grass and the bugs crawling around on my arms," Felix said, slowly turning to Cuthbert. "Here we have jobs and four walls around us. We're a part of something here. That has to be worth something, doesn't it?"

"It might not be what you think. You swapped the grass and the wind and the insects for oppidan delirium."

Felix shrugged and tried to move away from the wall, tripping over his foot.

"You'll get used to it eventually, if you want to," Cuthbert explained. "By then, you won't even have to think about getting up and working — it'll be as easy as breathing to you. It's how you have to act when you live like this. The first rule of living in a town — the clock always comes first. Just try to remember what you're a part of," Cuthbert said with a sigh, hopping out of the window.

Felix blinked a few times as he prepared to face the workday. His eyes were slow to adjust to each new shred of light from under the door as morning approached, unsure of whether he was awake or asleep until Mr. Slack banged on the door, telling him to get up for work.

* * *

When Felix entered the front of the shop, Mr. Slack stood behind the counter with a frown.

"Dominic really knows how to grind my gears," he said, reaching into a cupboard behind him. "He wants you to register — apparently it's what we do with new residents. There haven't been any new residents that anyone can remember, so I just have to take his word for it."

He dropped a piece of paper on the counter.

"You're going to have to fill out these forms and deliver them after closing today. It's absurd but I guess that's what you get with someone like Dominic Holsapple in charge. Wouldn't be surprised if this were some petty way of getting back at me. Well, say goodbye to your discount, buddy."

Felix glanced down at the paper in front of him. There were spaces for a date and place of birth — among other things that Felix either never had or couldn't recall. Mr. Slack folded his arms, tapping his finger against his elbow and waiting for Felix to finish the form. Felix decided to put down a pair of guesses. The information was plausible, even if it probably wasn't entirely accurate.

"Why does the town have two names?" Felix asked suddenly, trying to start a conversation. "I noticed that when I came in."

"It used to be two towns way back," Mr. Slack replied, keeping an eye on the form as Felix finished writing. "But Avaramck couldn't support itself so it joined with Doufsanctville to make the township — that's how it goes out here sometimes when business gets rough. We only get a small amount of support from the Republic. Sometimes, I wonder when everyone's going to up and leave this place. We're talking about a place where one side of town has maybe nine thousand people and another with maybe five — even with the township all joined up together and cozy like this, Doufsie is puny."

Without another word, Felix tore open the first line of boxes that came into view. After a few more were opened and their contents were placed onto the shelf, the morning had pushed to lunch.

Felix ran to the diner only to find that it had taken five minutes to get there from the department store. The restaurant's special for the day — a chicken sandwich for seven lire — stood out to him immediately. He bought the sandwich and sat, enjoying the brief pause in the day. When he finished half of his sandwich, he turned to the clock on the wall — he had only eight minutes left. He thought for a moment about Cuthbert, wondering where he had gone as he wrapped the other half of the sandwich in a napkin and hurried back to the department store.

He found Cuthbert sitting on the side of a street — with a minute to spare on his break. Felix handed him the other half of the sandwich from the diner.

"I was only hungry enough for half," Felix said, unpacking another box. "You can eat it if you want it."

"Thanks," Cuthbert said, putting the sandwich in his pocket. "I already ate, but I'm sure to get hungry later."

"You ate? Where did you go?"

"Well, the nice thing about fields is that they never close — they charge very little too."

Felix chuckled and hurried back to work.

* * *

He found Mr. Slack standing at the counter, annoyed. "Alright, lunch is over," he said with his hands on his hips. "Get back to work."

The afternoon crept by far slower than the morning. Felix worked in silence, sensing from Mr. Slack's demeanour that all friendly conversation had already been exhausted. He struggled to keep himself from falling asleep as the final hours of the day pushed through the store. He wiped his eyes often, and his legs became weak — when the day finally ended, Felix only had enough energy to return to his bed and sleep again.

Although he was tired, Felix still found his sleep interrupted repeatedly. He squirmed and writhed on the straw mattress, struggling for hours at a time to go back to sleep.

When Felix was finally rested enough to stand once more, the sun had set. He considered going to the bar again, but he decided swiftly against the idea — the threat of another encounter with Holsapple loomed in his mind. He thought about telling Cuthbert about the money he now owed to the town guard. Cuthbert had apparently escaped the notice of everyone in the town. He dismissed the idea and decided that Cuthbert was probably in even worse trouble with Holsapple than he was.

Felix nodded off and slept there until the next morning — he had been asleep for eight hours and felt ready to return to work.

Mr. Slack stood at the front grinning — his smile faded as he turned to Felix. Mr. Slack opened the doors and handed Felix a handful of money without making eye contact. Felix put the money in his pocket and quickly resumed unpacking boxes. Before long, all the items from the storage were safely placed on the shelves. Felix stood in the back, waiting for Mr. Slack to finish with a customer.

Felix shrugged and narrowed his brow. When Mr. Slack had sent the customer away, he scurried into the back, furiously raising his hands before his sweating face.

"What are you standing around for? There's work to do up front!"

"Sorry, sir. I've finished with the boxes, and you were with a customer."

"Right, so you thought you'd just stand around and waste time? You're a special kind of moron, aren't you? Maybe I should put up a sign so you remember to breathe too. Get to the front and mop up the floor. This place is disgusting."

"Yes, sir."

"The customers can handle you washing the floor," he explained. "It's much less worrying than you handling the stock — as good a job as you're doing, someone like you handling the stock is still cause for alarm right now. They'll only imagine you stealing it. You can clean, though — outsiders cleaning is fine. That work suits you."

Partway through Mr. Slack's sentence, the door to the store

swung open. Felix was ready to turn and leave for the back of the store until Mr. Slack stopped him with an outstretched hand. Felix felt his heart drop with dread as Holsapple entered the store with his giant bullmastiff walking at his side and slobbering onto the floor.

"How many times do I have to tell you?" Mr. Slack said, rushing to confront Holsapple. "Leave that mutt outside — it's drooling all over the floor I just cleaned."

"You mean the floor your boy just cleaned. I know Gulliver Slack to be many things and diligent has never been one of them." Holsapple turned to Felix. "Alright, kid, time to pay up. You held out yesterday, so I need double now — just the rules."

Felix stood, remembering the thirty-nine lire he still had left from the day before. "Are you deaf? Thirty-two lire on the counter, now!"

"Thirty-two?" Felix protested. "I thought you said five."

"You're not in who-cares-land anymore, kid. In Doufsie, when you hold out, it's fifteen percent interest every week."

Felix turned to Mr. Slack, who shrugged. "The hell are you looking at me for?" He said. "It's not my fault you skipped payments.

"What, do you want me to waste my time and resources telling you about your responsibilities? Though I'm not sure you've calculated that right, Dominic."

"Shut up, Gulliver. What do you care?"

Felix sighed and put the money on the counter. Holsapple took the money and put it in his pocket. As he reached to the counter to buy a bag of dog food, Felix felt the attention of the room divert from him, and he went back to mopping the floor, the hound's slobber dripping as soon as he mopped it up, but at least it kept him looking busy.

Once Holsapple left, Felix again went to Mr. Slack and asked him for a task.

"Did you grow up in a bed and breakfast or something?" Mr. Slack said. "I run the store, and you help me — there's plenty to do back here, so if you can't find something to do, you aren't looking hard enough."

With a hesitant nod, Felix went to the back of the store. He paced around the store for nearly an hour before he found a dirty counter to clean — the grime was almost a relief when he saw it. He wiped the dirt from the counter until it shone back at him.

* * *

Felix stared at the ceiling. His mind went blank, but some unseen force kept him from falling asleep.

Felix said nothing, watching his chest puff in and out until a sudden, damp flick fell upon his forehead. Felix sat up and wiped the water from his head. He looked up at the ceiling and saw a crack leaking above his bed. He plugged the leak with a handful of paper, but the drips continued as he tried to sleep.

Felix turned to his side and thought of going back to the plains. The urge to return to the road overwhelmed him until he recentered his mind and felt the blankets of the bed and the mattress beneath him. He remembered the cold nights on the grass and the chill of the wind — and decided that he would remain despite the irritating drip. Once more, he drifted in and out of rest — only this transition worsened with his growing awareness of the drips above.

STROLL

FELIX FOUND IT IMPOSSIBLE TO SLEEP. He pushed himself out of bed and briefly considered plugging the leak again, but decided it was pointless. It had grown since he last remembered — maybe a week, though it could have easily been two. He stepped outside into the dark, rubbing his head only to find it had gone dry at some point. He couldn't remember for certain.

Aside from a few shadows and echoes of muted laughter, it was silent in the early mornings of Doufsanctville & Avaramck. Even before dawn, Felix's presence roaming the streets was met with dimly lit scowls.

He continued wandering aimlessly. His feet guided him to Cuthbert sitting under a streetlamp. Felix started to turn away, only for Cuthbert to look up and meet his glance.

"Can't sleep again?" Cuthbert shouted from across the street. With a shrug, Felix approached him.

"You haven't told me how you've stayed in this town without anyone noticing you," he said, sitting next to Cuthbert on the side of the road.

"I didn't know you were still wondering," he replied with a grin. "But it's not that complicated — there's no magic — I just don't call too much attention to myself. Eventually, I just blend into the streets. You announced your arrival. That was your first mistake."

Felix slowly nodded and looked to the ground. "This sickness you were talking about," he started, following his thoughts. "Why aren't you affected by it?"

Cuthbert shrugged.

"I was at one time," he explained. "Oppidan delirium was just a normal way of life for me at one time. One day, I decided to go to the meadow. Slowly, it taught me how to survive. After a while, the oppidan delirium went away — now when I come back, I don't feel it anymore."

"Why come back at all, then?"

"It's getting harder to live on the plains. New towns form, the water gets polluted and the plants I can eat grow fewer all the time. Here, I can at least get a few coins and some fresh water from time to time until I find somewhere new to stay. People always end up feeling less generous after a while, though. I've never seen it happen so fast as it did here."

"I don't understand you, Cuthbert."

"I'm telling you: I go to a new town and people are happy to help me, but they always stop after a while. It took three months in that hamlet where you found me before no one gave me even a scrap — the town was just three days old when I arrived. But here, in this town, it's different. I don't know if it's because it's older or what, but the people have never given me anything."

"And why should they?" Felix suddenly snapped. "If you had any sense, you'd get a job instead of sitting around here all day."

"That would be the oppidan delirium talking," Cuthbert sighed. Felix stood up. "You came to me, Felix. You gave me water then and you brought me a sandwich here. You aren't like those soldiers — you're not even like the people in this town. It's not too late for you, but you have to get out of here."

Felix spun around and shoved Cuthbert.

"No, you need to stop trying to get into my head. I give you one sandwich and now suddenly you know me? Suddenly you know what's best for me? You're just a crazy beggar."

Felix scoffed and walked away, trying to ignore the pit in his stomach as he left Cuthbert to sit up and dust off his rags. By the time Felix arrived at the shop, it was daybreak again and he had to get back to work.

VISITOR

ANOTHER WEEK PASSED IN THE TOWN without Felix noticing. When it dawned on him that he had spent the days scraping by with what little lire he earned in the store — and what little remained after paying Holsapple each week — he felt his heart throb pain in his chest. Mr. Slack's wages were inconsistent. He wondered if Mr. Slack was even accounting for rent.

Felix had learned coveted tricks to save money. He only went to the diner for lunch every other day and when he ordered lunch, he always asked for the chicken sandwich and rationed it to last him for two meals. This strategy for saving money meant that Felix always had an extra few lire that he could hide under his pillow in case of emergency — which would normally contribute to paying off Holsapple. In weeks when Mr. Slack paid him little, Felix hid from Holsapple in his room at night or avoided him on the street.

As he worked one day, Felix started to add the numbers together. He fell to the side and caught himself on the counter, wondering how he had spent so long in Doufsie without noticing. He realized that he had no way of knowing how much money he had earned since arriving nor how much Mr. Slack had taken from him.

He straightened himself up as Mr. Slack walked by, narrowly avoiding yet another remark from the shop owner's jeering wit. Felix stayed silent outside of the moments when he spoke to customers or when he was asked a direct question by Mr. Slack. Felix even stayed silent when he counted his wages one day to find that Mr. Slack had taken too much for his rent. Fearing eviction, he kept quiet and tried to stretch his money further through the week.

He saw Cuthbert on occasion since the stroll, but Felix began passing him by without saying a word.

Felix ran to the counter and started helping another customer — Amaria Swerfard, the town nurse. One by one, he learned the names of each of the inhabitants in the town. None of them seemed to like him but they tolerated his existence as long as he helped out in the store.

"You contribute something to this town at least," Swerfard said as she bagged her purchases. "That's more than can be said for some people out there."

Felix nodded. "I'm proud to serve the people of Doufsie, ma'am."

Mr. Slack glanced toward Felix as Swerfard left the store. Silent approval radiated from him as the door slammed shut. Felix turned back to his work until the lunch hour came once again.

Before he knew it, Felix sat in the diner, glancing over his shoulder as he shuffled the sandwich into a small container he borrowed from the store for such occasions until he washed it and returned it to the shelf. When the container he used was purchased, he simply borrowed another.

Either Mr. Slack didn't notice or — more likely — didn't care, but the container remained a vital part of the plan nonetheless. Once, Felix had tried to carry fries in his pocket only for them to lose their shape and grow bloated and inedible from the moisture in the linen. When he had to throw out the fries, he felt a twinge of embarrassment that lingered in his chest and reminded him to bring the container.

The diner's owner, Steven Stoltzfus was a large, softly spoken man who knew how to mind his own business. Felix knew, on several occasions, he had directly observed him swiping fries into a greasy glass container — each time, Stoltzfus simply looked away. Yet, Felix continued to look over his shoulder, anticipating that someone might find some way to use his siphoning against him.

On the rare occasion when Stoltzfus spoke, he said only a few words at a time. "Done?" he asked, gesturing to Felix's plate.

Felix nodded and Stoltzfus took the plate away, disappearing into the kitchen once more. Felix stood up to go back to work. The lunch hour had gradually become shorter as the weeks had pushed forward — now, Felix barely noticed when the hour hand of the clock announced that he had to return to the store.

* * *

The final hours of the day remained slow and painful — most of the traffic in the store was in the morning and the later hours of the afternoon were left uneventful save for the odd visit from townspeople working late.

One afternoon, Felix struggled to keep his eyes open when the sound of distant cheering caught his attention. Startled, he checked the back for Mr. Slack, only to find him standing with his hands on his hips.

"Come on now," he said. "What are you doing here? We're getting a visit from him."

"Who?"

"Who? I guess you really haven't been here very long, have you? John, the Consul of Doufsie, is paying us a visit — he's our founder. He's a great speaker, and if you want to live here, this is a rare event that'll tell you everything you need to know about us. It's really something."

"What about the store?"

"Forget it, we're closed early. No one's coming in here at a time like this."

Mr. Slack eagerly marched out of the store, brandishing a camera. Felix followed at a distance into the streets where he joined the clamouring crowd that had amassed in the streets. Felix stood in awe of the scene as he walked forward with the flow of the marching bodies — normally, the streets were bustling and controlled, but now, they were filled with cheering and a rush that seemed foreign and unnatural.

The noise heightened as a strange figure came into view — a bald man stood atop a stone podium in the centre of the town, holding a pair of caterpillars above his head before a golden statue in his image. Felix looked away as the face of John Wotan Clempner came into view.

"This is the last line!" his voice called. "The future belongs to us, my friends."

"Doufsie is the last chance our civilization has! Through the beautiful gift of agriculture, you have all risen above your surroundings and carved a great community out of a vast, untamed wilderness. You are all heroes. When time's arrow comes at last for the great cities of the Republic — for Vasta, for Magnum, for Cartago, for Dagastay and even for our beloved capital for which this great Republic is named — I will be at ease because The Township of Doufsanctville & Avaramck will be standing firm.

"Just a few months ago, time's arrow came for a kingdom that dared to stand against us. Its coward king fled underground and the city fell to our great legions. But the people of Doufsie know the direction of history. You stand with Emperor Crosigk von Pearson in his eternal struggle for survival in this miserable world of pain! God bless this place and all of its people! May it never die!"

The people in the crowd cheered and threw flowers toward John Wotan Clempner as he threw his arms up into the air and tossed some caterpillars onto the ground before him. Mr. Slack snapped several pictures — coming out of a bizarre trance that had been holding him still as a spectator of the moment.

"Let these sublime creatures show us the way — the fortress is nearly complete and soon the blond beast will come to us. O, what hope you give me! This place will soon be the temple of our second saviour! The great coming is upon us and you are the threshold guardians at its gates."

Another round of applause followed, and John Wotan Clempner bowed. He rose again with a grin and waved his hands to dismiss the crowd. The town let out a final cheer before returning to their daily lives.

As the crowd departed, John Wotan Clempner was already marching toward Felix — when Felix turned back to Mr. Slack, he was grinning with an outstretched hand.

"It's such a great honour to meet you, Mr. Clempner," he said. "Please let me know if there's anything I can do for you."

John Wotan Clempner stopped for a moment, stroking his bald head. "Well, there is one thing you can do for me — I need more supplies. I understand that you run a department store here in town?"

Mr. Slack eagerly nodded and led John Wotan Clempner, beckoning Felix to follow with a frantic gesture from his hand. Felix complied, even as his feet were reluctant to move. He turned back to the caterpillars — after having been on the ground for only a few short moments, they had already eaten a quarter of the grass that had been growing in the middle of the town, leaving the hard earth from where they sprouted to dry out with no foliage.

* * *

In a manic silence, Mr. Slack took John Wotan Clempner into the store and threw the door open with a performative gusto that Felix had never seen before. He invited the bald man inside and, reluctantly, Felix followed them into the store. He found John Wotan Clempner grabbing random items in a rush of motion as Mr. Slack took a series of rapid photos.

By the time he left — without paying — the bald man had taken half of the store's stock. "The store looks empty now, what are we going to sell?" Felix asked.

"Forget that! These pictures are going to make us rich by the time I photocopy them. Clempner himself stood just behind you and I have the proof — the original for the wall and some copies for the customers. Oh Christ, kid, why do you look so grouchy in that picture? It's unattractive. No matter. We can crop you out, I'm sure. Just take the photos to the studio on the corner — you know, where old Catia Bierhals works?"

Felix nodded as Mr. Slack passed him the camera and some change. "Who is that guy anyway?" Felix asked, worried for the answer.

Mr. Slack dropped the camera on the counter and marched toward Felix.

"John Wotan Clempner," he began, taking a deep breath, "founded Doufsanctville. He generously joined it with Avaramck when that township was failing. Somehow he's over a hundred years old — would you believe it? He's a great man who makes regular visits here — he has a mansion uptown, but he rarely goes there since he's so busy travelling with his caterpillars. Rumour has it, he bred the creatures himself. That man and his brilliance are what makes this town so rich."

"But you told me that Doufsie is broke."

"Did I? Well, it can feel like that sometimes, but a bad day in the Republic is a good day anywhere else in the world. I must have let my mood get the better of me — it's important to remember that this is the greatest nation on earth. Anyway, Clempner's birthday is coming up. You'll love it — there's a huge festival and everyone comes to celebrate. I guess he came for a little pre-birthday welcome home? Ah well, I'm sure the man had his reasons. You don't get to a hundred-and-forty-four without a good set of brains in your noggin. Have you noticed how healthy and articulate he is for his age? If only you and me could have even half the wits he does. If the world thought like John Wotan Clempner, it would be a much finer place. That's for sure. Anyway, get those photos printed. I want to start selling them immediately — as soon as we reopen."

Mr. Slack whistled a merry tune as he went upstairs. Felix sighed and the clock struck the end of his shift. He wandered into the street, distraught by the city's returning patron.

Felix slowly walked around as people bustled and chatted about the visit from John Wotan Clempner — all except one conversation between Amaria Swerfard the nurse and Richard Atterton the bartender. The pair could be found gossiping in the quieter corners of the street as they smoked but it had been some time since Felix had witnessed them directly.

"Apparently, it was his car," Atterton said, taking a draw from his cigarette. "They found a tunnel. It's smart; they followed his route to church. They must have been at it for months. Everyone else in the car was killed."

"Is that right?" Swerfard replied, her eyes anxiously scanning the street. "Who was in there with him?"

"Driver and a bodyguard it sounds like. It's unbelievable that Crosigk made it out alive. He's one lucky devil."

"Yeah," Swerfard nodded, her tone somewhat removed from her words as her eyes fell on Felix. "It's a miracle he survived."

"Crazy thing is that they tried to finish him off with a gun, but it jammed. The guy ran off, but the emperor apparently emerged from the car and tried to run after him despite his injuries."

"Is that right?" Swerfard said again, jabbing Atterton and gesturing to Felix as he passed by. "What a brave man the emperor is to chase his attackers in that state. I'd hate to lose a man so great as that."

Atterton suddenly straightened up.

"That's right," he said. "We're lucky to have such a great leader. I'd hate to lose him."

Felix turned away, trying to forget that he had overheard the conversation — it was the standard courtesy he paid the pair as he heard them gossip. It was clear that they never wanted to be heard. He turned the corner and found the photography store as the voices of Atterton and Swerfard faded into the air.

He opened the door to the shop and Ms. Catia Bierhals looked up from the counter, peering at him through a pair of crooked spectacles that rested on her nose.

"Hello, Felix,," she said. "I didn't think you were the type for photography."

"I'm not usually," Felix replied, placing the camera on the counter. "I just have some pictures from Mr. Slack. They're of John Wotan Clempner — he visited our shop just a little while ago."

Ms. Bierhals nodded and took the camera.

"Oh, what a lovely occasion," she said. "I'd be happy to develop those for you."

"I also need you to crop me out," Felix added. "Mr. Slack says I look too glum — it spoils the mood of the photograph I suppose. Silly error. It's my resting face. I didn't know I was being photographed."

Ms. Bierhals nodded, and Felix said his thanks, putting the money from Mr. Slack on the counter as he turned to leave.

DROWNING

ANOTHER EXHAUSTING DAY, another exhausting night. Felix had learned to wake up partway through his sleep and get dressed for the day, sitting on the bed and leaning against the wall as he slept until morning. When he would get up off the floor, Felix immediately would go to work.

One morning he entered the store, Felix found the counter empty and unattended. With a sigh, Felix searched for Mr. Slack, only to find him gone. He sat at the counter, waiting for the shop to open — an hour passed before any customers came into the store. An old woman quietly slipped in through the door from the quiet, empty streets. She went to the counter and leaned over to meet Felix's eye.

"What are you doing here?" she snapped. "You were supposed to follow your shadow. I hoped that my suppositions were wrong — yet here you are, working in some department store instead of finding your destiny."

"Do I know you?"

"Know me? I saved you from drowning. I'm old — it's my memory that should be fading, not yours. What will happen when you die in this town before you figure out who you are? Are you prepared for that kind of regret?"

The words lingered and billowed in the air. Felix stood back, watching his mouth peel open and his eyes narrow. He sighed and wiped his eyes, suddenly unsure if he were awake. He took a deep breath and turned back to the old woman.

"Ma'am, If you're not buying anything, I'm afraid you'll have to leave."

"I had such faith in you as well. If you ever remember what you're supposed to be doing and who you're supposed to be, I'll be on the other side of the woods. I can't waste my time telling you the obvious — they're expecting me back there."

Shaking her head, the old woman went back into the street and disappeared. Felix let the confusion leave him as he forgot the woman's face. Soon, there was another small flock of customers to be served — soon after Ms. Swerfard and Ms. Tania Yolland, the town's school teacher, had left, lunch hour arrived once more.

Felix had the fries he had siphoned from the diner. He sat, eating in silence as he waited for Mr. Slack to return. When the day ended and there was still no sign of Mr. Slack, Felix closed the store and went to sleep, making sure the door at the back of the building was still open for Mr. Slack when he finally returned.

Only partway through waking up, getting dressed and leaning against the wall for the remaining hours of the night did Felix remember that he had missed yet another payment to Holsapple.

Mr. Slack pounded on the door, interrupting Felix's unsteady sleep. Felix stood up and opened the door, already dressed once again.

"I was out yesterday — I meant to tell you — since the day of the festival for Clempner's birthday is in two days and many preparations need to be made. Or rather, it was in two days yesterday. Of course, now it's tomorrow. We have a lot of work that needs to be done. It's a very special day for us, you understand. You were alright here by yourself, weren't you?"

Felix shrugged and got to work, following Mr. Slack's instructions closely, even as his mind remained distant. Felix cleaned until no dust remained on the floor. When Mr. Slack was satisfied, he told Felix to add several decorations in celebration of John Wotan

Clempner — posters, large sparkling letters and a sign just above the register adorned with the bald man's portrait. Mr. Slack looked with pride at the decorated store.

"Clempner will be so glad when he sees what I have done for him," he beamed. "Oh, look at how I've decorated my store for the greatest man who has ever lived on this planet. And nice job cropping those pictures. They look much better."

* * *

Felix turned to the streets and saw similarly decorated shops. He wandered out of the shop and saw every streetlamp adorned with pictures of John Wotan Clempner with messages proclaiming his unique and unending greatness. Felix could only stand in awe — with a slight hint of disgust — of the display and the town's commitment to the image of the bald man. He remembered that John Wotan Clempner had abandoned him to be devoured by an army of caterpillars after giving a grating, repetitive, inescapable speech and he wondered how such a man could be so beloved by so many in the town.

The sound of a distant barking dog reminded Felix why he had been staying in the store. He turned to go back inside, but a shout from the approaching Holsapple made him stand in place.

"No, not this time, kid! You're not skipping out on this payment now! Either you give me sixty-three lire now, or you lose your legs — it'll be so fun to watch you crawl out of here on your hands with two bleeding stumps dragging behind you! Actually, I hope you don't have my money just so that I can enjoy the sight. Please tell me you're out of money so I can laugh. I haven't laughed in a very long time."

"I do have the money," Felix replied, facing Holsapple. "But you aren't getting it."

"If that's what you want!"

Holsapple prepared to release his snarling dog — only when Felix sighed indifferently did he pull the animal back.

"You don't do anything, do you?" he said, looking Holsapple in the eyes. "You just press me — and possibly others — for money you can't even earn yourself. You run around with your giant, stupid dog and try to forget what you know."

"And what's that, then?"

"Think about it, Holsapple — you're a leech. You don't contribute anything to the town, and your job only wastes our resources. So, if you want to have that stupid dog bite off my legs, go ahead, but it won't change anything. Sooner or later, people will realize that you're out of touch, and they'll find a better guard who does more to keep them safe."

A crowd had amassed during the argument. Many from the town had gathered in the streets, watching intently as Felix spoke against Holsapple — an action he hadn't observed from anyone since he had arrived in the town. After a pause, the onlookers erupted in applause — Felix stood tall and nodded as Holsapple backed down and slowly backed away into the crowd.

When the applause quieted, Felix still felt a feeling of pride and belonging — the money in his pocket would remain for no reason other than his fast and affirmed wit. He had earned it and it belonged to him more than it did to Holsapple or anyone else.

After the store closed, he went directly to the bar. When he arrived, Felix found the same band playing, and he dropped several lire into their hat before descending into a seat.

"Hey, Rick! Hey Rick," Felix said, frantically trying to get the bartender's attention. "Give me a whisky and leave the bottle here. I've got more than enough money to pay for it. When I'm done with it, bring another. I don't want to see the bottom of my glass."

"Works for me," the bartender replied, pouring. "But I'm cutting you off if you get rowdy."

"Oh, I'll behave myself, don't you worry Ricky. I'm all good for it."

With a raised eyebrow, the bartender dropped a bottle of whisky onto the counter and tended to other guests.

"Hey!" Felix called out, throwing his arms excitedly into the air. "Don't any of you ever say Ricky Atterton isn't good for it! Best man in Doufsie right here!"

As the band started to play, Felix let a smile creep onto his face. He sang along to the music in a wild, off-key bellow as the night faded into his memory.

FESTIVAL

FELIX AWOKE TO A QUIET BAR and an empty pocket. He searched for the lire he had earned from working the day before but found only lint. He stood up and felt a stinging headache pour into his temples as he stumbled into a jagged path. The headache turned to nausea, and he knelt over the sink behind the bar to vomit, but nothing came from his mouth. The feeling remained. He returned heavily and painfully to the ground and started to fish for the lost money, but there was nothing on the floor but carpet and spilled alcohol.

As he glanced around the bar, he felt a wave of relief that he was alone. He sat on the ground, leaning against the counter. He stayed there until he had the strength to stand. His thoughts lingered on his empty pocket as he wondered whether he had spent or lost the money.

When pain shot through his temple again, he stopped wondering.

"Hey, Babimoosay," a voice called from the bar. "Get off the floor. I have sweeping to do." Felix looked up and saw Atterton staring down at him. Slowly, he stood up and dusted himself off.

"Look at the state of you," Atterton said, scoffing. "I mean, I kept offering you water, and you kept telling me no, so here we are."

"Yeah, yeah," Felix replied, swatting at the air. "Did you see where my money went? I could have sworn I had some left. The tall guy from the store didn't pay me a visit and swipe the money, did he? Or was it Slack?"

"No, nobody came," Atterton said, flicking his broom across the floor. "It's in the register. You gave me every last lire you had until you passed out."

Felix nodded, slightly irritated that the simplest explanation had proven the truest.

"I've never seen anyone drink so much whisky. Your liver's not going to be happy with you in a few years' time when you aren't so young anymore."

"Good thing it's now, then," Felix replied, stumbling slowly toward the door and the streets. "I live for now."

* * *

He returned to the store only to find Mr. Slack turning on the open sign. He saw Felix and furrowed his brow angrily.

"Where have you been?" He spat, pushing the door open. "The festival's about to start, and I need another man at the counter here. Get inside and stop screwing around."

"Yes, sir."

With a deep breath, Mr. Slack stepped aside and showed Felix into the store. The bright, sparkling letters that decorated the store walls worsened his headache — Felix clenched his teeth through every pang.

Customers flocked, but Felix couldn't tell them apart and only focused on their orders, only to forget them and move on to the next person in line.

The day was slow and felt impossibly long. Through the fog of his headache and the traffic of the store, Felix had no way of knowing how many hours remained in the day. When Mr. Slack finally told him that the workday was over early since the festival had begun, Felix only had the energy to notice that the stock of candles had run out. He slumped to lie down so his head might finally calm itself, but he could only alleviate half the pain before Mr. Slack pulled him to his feet.

"Get off the ground. What's wrong with you? The festival's starting — we are so lucky to share an epoch with the world's greatest man, but you don't know anything! You're too busy sitting on the floor to see how good you've got it!"

"My head hurts, sir. I need to rest."

Mr. Slack silenced Felix with a slap that sent him to the floor. He shook his head as he stood above him momentarily before yanking him back to his feet.

"Fine, fine," Felix huffed, and Mr. Slack released him.

"You'll be thanking me in a few minutes," Mr. Slack said. "This festival is really something, I'd hate for you to miss it."

* * *

Felix walked through the lively streets of the town. A parade had formed and Mr. Slack quickly followed it to the square.

The statue of John Wotan Clempner that stood in the middle of the town shone in the light of the sun as it came into view. It was carefully decorated with an ajar birthday hat on its newly polished head. Just beside the statue was a wooden platform with people crowding around its base and chattering excitedly among themselves.

Felix's headache still stung — it wasn't as painful as it had been before, but with each word of chatter from the townspeople, the rhythmic throbbing worsened.

He heard an eruption of loud cheering as footsteps crossed the stage. He turned to see John Wotan Clempner standing up top and waving to the cheering crowd as he prepared to speak. Felix grimaced — he longed for the applause to continue, rendering his speech impossible.

"Thank you, thank you," he said, motioning with his hands. "Yesterday, I was sad to leave this great township, and I was elated to return this morning. That's the great power of Doufsie — every time I see this town, it feels like the first time I've seen my plans completed.

"I founded this town nearly eighty years ago. To say it aloud makes me feel very strange — like I've become something more than the human I was born as. I only hope you can all ascend with me to this great level.

"In all my years shaping this wild, lawless land into the great society that you now all enjoy, I have learned only one thing — history is an image cast in constant, living change. It is our duty to master its patterns of change and to outlast them for we are the first people in the world to even have the possibility to do so. We have the wherewithal and the drive that none before us held and we can actually see the future.

"This isn't to disparage our ancestors — and those who live like our ancestors — for they, unlike us, have been unspoiled by the cost of progress that we must pay. We have chosen to do evil for the greater good and they — bless them — had no such knowledge.

"My dream is that we can break this too and become people of knowledge and goodness. Once more, we are the only people in the entire history of everything that has ever been who are even capable of pursuing such an endeavour!"

The crowd cheered loudly again, and Felix felt his ears ring. He hurried away from the crowd and sat still, letting his headache turn again to nausea before relief. He had found himself again entranced by Clempner — had he not been frozen by his pain, he would have left the festival far earlier. He felt his head and let the relief expand into his chest.

"You alright?" asked a voice. Felix turned — Cuthbert had emerged from the crowd.

"I'm fine. I'm just —" as Felix stood, the sounds of the festival echoing behind him, he noticed a small figure in the distance. He ran closer to see the rough shape of a person approaching the town from the flat plains. Confused, he held up a hand and waved only for the distant figure to remain still — the silhouette's eyes grimly glowing.

"What is it?" Cuthbert asked, seeing the figure.

"We have to get out of here," Felix replied, his eyes growing wide with terror. "Don't let him see you."

Suddenly, a pair of hands threw Felix to the ground.

"Alright, kid," Holsapple said, pinning Felix to the ground. "No one to save you now. That's the last time you get to humiliate me like that. Now, last chance … "

Cuthbert pushed Holsapple aside and stood between him and Felix. "You don't need to do that, Dominic." He puffed his chest out, planting his feet.

Holsapple twisted his face in confusion. "Who are you? How do you know my name?"

"We met a few times in the town," Cuthbert said. "You really don't remember? You wanted to—"

Holsapple shook his head and stepped forward. When Cuthbert reached out to stop him, Holsapple threw him against a wall. With a sudden thwack, Cuthbert fell motionless and slumped to the ground. Felix watched in shock, turning back to Holsapple.

"I don't have any more money," Felix pleaded, his voice trembling as he turned to Cuthbert. "I spent it all. I swear, it's the truth. I swear."

"Well, I guess you know what that means. Sorry, kid, but that dog doesn't feed herself." Holsapple locked a set of handcuffs to link Felix's wrist to a sewer grate. With a grin, he stood up to approach his growling bullmastiff who stood tied to a lamppost under the delicately placed portrait of John Wotan Clempner.

He reached down to untie the leash as a booming voice sounded from the distance. "I'll take it from here, sir. The empire thanks you for your service."

"What the … " Holsapple spluttered. "Where the hell did all you people come from? What's with all these new faces?"

Felix turned to see the man with the loud voice holding an identification card. As an argument ensued, Felix wriggled desperately against the handcuffs.

"I'm here for the fugitive, for Gussie over there."

"Gussie? Who on earth is that? Not this guy — this is Felix Cabil Babimoosay. He's under the jurisdiction of The Township of

Doufsanctville & Avaramck. Are you with that guy over there?"

"There's been a mistake. Perhaps he's lied to you. His name is August Orosius. I'm telling you, he's wanted by the empire for — "

"And I'm telling you, I have no idea who that is. If you're taking the kid anywhere, you'd better pay up. I expect to be compensated fairly. I did my civic duty to the empire too after all."

"You will be — after he's handed in."

"Sorry, pal, that doesn't work for me. How do I know you won't just run off with him and leave me out to dry?"

The man with the loud voice glared into Holsapple's eyes, turning to face him with irritation burning in the glow of his glance.

"Now, I want answers damnit," Holsapple said. "Who are you people and what are you doing in Doufsie?"

With a sigh, the man with the loud voice grabbed Holsapple by the throat and violently tossed him into a nearby shop window. He crouched next to Felix and silently removed the handcuffs with a set of pliers. He hoisted Felix up and led him forcefully by the shoulder. Felix turned to Cuthbert as he lay in the street, his hair matted with blood.

Thinking in a sudden rush, Felix slipped Holsapple's dog loose from its rope. Startled by the growling dog, the man with the loud voice loosened his grip enough that Felix could break free. Felix ran blindly toward the festival. The angered dog chased after him. After passing a few streets, he heard the footsteps of the man with the loud voice following close behind.

The festival crowd was unbothered by the scene — John Wotan Clempner enraptured the audience as his speech continued. Felix turned back and swiftly kicked the dog away with an irked grunt. The mastiff let out a sharp whimper as she stumbled, panting. The man with the loud voice gained on him as he turned to the crowd.

"Hey!" Felix called, but he too was drowned out by John Wotan Clempner's speech. "Get inside! Inside! He'll kill you!"

The crowd remained unmoved until Felix darted into the centre of the plaza and caused a disturbance as he fell to the ground. The few discombobulated utterances soon turned to screams as the dog charged toward Felix. Before it could reach Felix prone, the man irritably snatched it by the hind legs and swung it into the far distance. He then stomped toward Felix. Mr. Slack, having seen the commotion, stood in front of the man's path.

"What are you doing?" he said. "What's going on?"

"Get out of the way."

"Are you from the empire? Are you a legionary? Please, what's — " Without another word, the man with the loud voice took his stolen imperial sword from his waist and cut Mr. Slack's throat. The shocked man fell to the ground, blood spurting from his neck as he lay, twitching the last of his life away. Several people in the crowd screamed as the man with the loud voice continued madly swatting his sword, sending red onto the grass and the pavement as his glowing eyes scanned the crowd of falling corpses for Felix.

Felix clambered to his feet and pushed his way through the chaos — John Wotan Clempner mindlessly disappeared off stage without a trace as the man with the loud voice lit a torch and threw it onto a nearby building. Soon, every roof in the centre of town was engulfed in flames and littered with dead bodies. Felix could hardly recognize anyone in the maimed state of the burning corpses.

Even through the tangled mess of blood and fire, Felix could make out some of the dead, like the motionless faces of Richard Atterton, the bartender and Amaria Swerfard, the nurse. He turned away, tears flooding from his eyes as he feared finding more familiar faces in the carnage.

He looked back to where Cuthbert had been lying in the street — only to find it empty. A pit settled in his stomach — half of relief, half of fear — as he hurried toward the outskirts of the town.

He searched the flames and the maimed mess of limbs that surrounded him for any trace of life. He ran wildly, searching in vain as the flames spread to the far reaches of the town. The blaze left only ash in its wake. As death and destruction flooded his eyes, Felix felt his feet grow tense. He stumbled backward and tripped over an arm severed from its owner. He desperately wondered who the arm had belonged to — he was certain he had met them during his time in Doufsanctville & Avaramck. At some point, he had met everyone. Many were gone now, either cut down and bleeding out or fleeing into the plains.

As the glowing eyes of the man with the loud voice emerged from the wreckage, Felix started backpedalling. When the man tried to charge at him, Felix stumbled, slamming his head against the stone pathway underfoot. Blood poured down his neck. Cuthbert emerged covered in blood, gripping a flaming plank, swinging wildly at the man with the loud voice — his sword chewing into the wood with every blow.

Felix watched the two men engage — Cuthbert struck the man with the loud voice repeatedly which only seemed to irritate him. Fragments splintered from the board until a wide swipe lodged the plank into the man's eye. He shrieked as blood poured down his face. Cuthbert readied for another strike as the man with the loud voice regained his balance.

Cuthbert howled and charged, but the man with the loud voice deflected his strike before disarming him. He pulled back his sword and stabbed him in two fluid motions. Cuthbert fell to the ground, the life fading from his eyes. The man with the loud voice retrieved his weapon from Cuthbert's chest.

Felix's heart sank as his glance locked on Cuthbert's lifeless body in the middle of the town — his polished boots lay motionless, the toes pointed stiffly toward the sun. Only when the man with the loud voice turned again did Felix find his feet and run desperately from Doufsanctville & Avaramck.

HUNT

FELIX RAN AIMLESSLY INTO THE HORIZON. The flames upon the ruins of Doufsanctville & Avaramck burned as bright as the evening sun, and their heat struck Felix's back as he dashed away, fearing that the man with the loud voice might again be close behind him. His thoughts kept turning to Cuthbert — hoping against all possibility that somehow he had survived the massacre.

He ran until he could no longer see the burning buildings behind him. He fell to his knees and caught his breath. His head started to spin sometime following his exit. He took a few deep breaths until the pain left his brow.

As Felix sat, his hands gently feeling the land beside him, he saw a distant shadow emerge from the light of the chaos. He turned, and the familiar silhouette of the man with the loud voice was upon him, blood pouring down the tightly clenched socket where his eye used to be. He lurched towards Felix, dust kicking up with every heavy stomp.

"You've run all this way," the man said. "It wasn't easy to find you, Gussie."

"You keep calling me that," Felix replied. "But you don't even care who I am — that my name is Felix Cabil Babimoosay — you don't care about anything except handing someone in. I just fit the description. You destroyed an entire town of people. Why?"

"Can't blame a man for making a living. To be honest, as I

followed the stream and your footprints for the past few days, I began to realize something — I don't think you are the guy I'm looking for. And that town — bloody Doufsanctville & Avaramck, Clempner's stupid pet — it was nothing more than a leech on the Republic. It was so expensive to maintain. Sure, I'll get lambasted, but really the emperor knows that I just did him a favour. Even Clempner — being an intelligent man — will come to realize that in time. Something as pure and as noble as the blond beast has no place in a filthy squalor like Doufsie — it will have to come to the capital instead."

The man grabbed Felix and pulled him to his feet. "You do seem to be telling the truth — that or experiencing some psychotic episode — but then I realized that it makes no difference at all. You do resemble the guy I was watching in prison. Anyway, to me, you are the guy I'm looking for because I've been chasing you, and when I bring you back, all this hubbub about the incompetent legion will die down enough to make the emperor relax. It's bad for the man's recovery. We've already had to report five soldiers missing, and that's got him quite rattled. I serve the emperor. If he's satisfied — which he will be — then I will be.

"But I must say, I never expected you to make it so far. I'm lucky I found you — maybe you're lucky too. I doubt you would have lasted long out here. All good things must come to an end, I'm afraid; justice has its price."

"What kind of justice is that?" Felix spat without thinking — the man's grip loosened as he formed an answer and Felix quickly devised a plan. "You dare say the word 'justice' when a man was murdered right in front of you — when you slaughtered all of those innocent people. You killed my friend."

"Well, you went to that town and you didn't hand yourself in. So, if we're being fair, Mr. Orosius, I think you'll find that you killed them. And your friend did attack me in the performance of my duties. He gouged out my eye with a wooden plank — it's a clear case of self-defence."

Felix felt his face contort in rage and guilt as his fists shook. The man with the loud voice grinned as he saw the storming emotions behind Felix's eyes.

"Justice is nothing more than an abstract concept to satisfy an inborn anxiety from when we are wronged. When a crime is committed, we want the person responsible punished — it's just human nature — but we can't always get what we want and it is the duty of those with the responsibility of power to quell the impotent cries of the rabid masses. I'm sure you understand that. Without us, you idiots would run around this entire world killing each other just because you can or because you don't like someone's face.

"Every invention, every advance in science and every second of peace in civilization is down to us alone. You're nothing more than a pathetic ingrate running around like this. You could never understand the full weight of what I do — what the emperor and his loyal heroes do. You would be lost without us — giving yourself up so that the world can keep turning safely is a small price to pay, August Orosius. You could have saved everyone in that town. Can you live with their blood on your hands?"

As the man spoke, Felix was able to step away from his grasp — he stood, letting the man with the loud voice finish speaking as he inched away. By the time the man had concluded, there was nearly a distance between them. Felix noted that his shadow pointed toward the man with the loud voice — as he finished speaking, the man lunged toward Felix to recapture him. He misjudged the distance between the shadow and Felix, slipped on the grasses and fought to catch himself.

Felix ran forward, following his shadow into the distance as the familiar chase ensued once more and carried him into the distance of the flat plains, constantly glancing over his shoulder for the glowing eye that pursued him.

IMPOSSIBLE FOREST

WHEN HE WAS REASONABLY CERTAIN that the man with the loud voice had been abandoned in the distance, Felix followed his shadow past the horizon of the dense plains. He found himself once more wandering blindly until he glanced at the ground and watched as a series of shadows danced before his eyes. When he had regained his bearings, he looked up and found himself lost in a dark forest.

His mind was distantly occupied by memories of Cuthbert — the sight of his lifeless body falling limp on the ground — but he tried not to dwell on the disembodied images, only fortifying them in his peripheral thought.

The forest — a scarce finding on the plains — had emerged from the horizon's depths and taken every direction with its width. Felix looked around and decided there was nothing to do but travel through the woods and find whatever the old woman had hoped would be waiting for him. Instantly, Felix wondered why the old woman had sent him to such an empty place.

The forest appeared as though it had been placed upon the plains by some careless hand — each tree was spaced evenly from its neighbours — originally, at least, though there had since been roots that had disrupted this original plan — and the ferns offered by these woods were not the same as the sparse trees that grew under the plain's blue skies. Felix walked with a raised eyebrow as he examined the strange wood. He continued walking until he realized that the wood had continuously stolen his direction sometime after he had wandered in.

He pressed on, hoping to find where he had dropped his way, only to find rows upon rows of empty trees. He began to grow tired, nearly drifting into sleep as he went.

A twig snapping resounded in the distance. Felix turned and saw a tall, thin beast that stood unlike anything he had seen before. Its shoulders were broad enough to block the light from the sun. Its skin was pale. On its limp body, it wore loose, ornate clothes sewn with care from a mahogany cloth not normally found on the plains that drifted in the light breeze. Its eyes burned with a sickening blue. On its head, several abrupt quills of yellow hair stood to outline the shape of its skull. It was squat and stubby like a box. Through white, pearly teeth, the beast snarled and uttered words of condescending gibberish.

Felix stood back and looked upon the beast, struggling to see how he might slip past. The beast took from its side a knife that glinted sharp and clear in the light. Felix ran back the way he came — or at least, what he could remember of getting to that place where the beast stood. He ran back and away, fast as he could through the trees. The beast never ceased its running; even as it began to tire in its breath, its speed persisted defiantly. As he ran, the man with the loud voice appeared on the path.

"That's enough," he said, grabbing Felix. "You're only making it worse for yourself. You want to end up like your buddy?"

Without thinking, Felix punched the man in his side abdomen to be let past; however, the beast finally stopped its charge and stood over them both. The man with the loud voice fell to his knees and a face of ecstasy crept onto his face.

"I've heard such stories of you," he said, his booming voice nearly cracking under his elation. "But I never thought I'd see your face with my own eyes — what a beauty you are."

The beast nodded, and the man with the loud voice stood to greet it.

Felix turned and continued his desperate sprint forward. The man with the loud voice followed close behind the beast, struggling to match its great speed.

Felix ran until the soil swallowed him, the beast chasing him even as he disappeared into the earth. As he fell, Felix saw the beast push the man with the loud voice with a look of apathy into the hole after him. The man fell faster and tumbled past Felix into the endless darkness of the pit.

Down, down he sank into the depths of the earth below him. He felt insects and rodents crawling on his face as the dirt flowed like a stream to a rock. Only Felix sank where a rock stands still and motionless in the river until time wears it down to a mere pebble.

As he plunged into the depths, Felix looked to his hand, flapping uselessly in the wind of the pit. He watched the dirt crumble around it, slowly turning into a distant, familiar sand. He landed in a heap and shook himself free of the sand. When he looked down to dust the sand from his clothes, he saw that the ground was closer to him than he recalled.

* * *

"Hurry up," A voice called. "You'll be late."

He turned to see a young boy of about thirteen years of age, standing against a landscape of sand on a mountain overlooking a vast span of marble buildings. Felix rushed to catch up with the boy — his legs moved of their own mind. As Felix's feet hurried down the dunes, he realized that he had somehow returned to a place he had avoided revisiting even as he had wandered through the flat plains. His role as a passive observer terrified him for reasons he could not explain.

The boy led him down the mountain to a small building at the centre of the town. A tall, thin man rang a bell, and a flock of children hurried inside. They sat upon stools in rows of seven, and Felix's legs took their place near the window at the back of the room. The other children inched away as he approached, their eyes turning to the floor in disgust.

The boy who had led Felix to the building turned back to him with a look of sympathy, only to stand to attention as the other children stood for the tall man's entrance.

"I swear to faithfully execute all that His Venerable Majesty, Emperor Leicester Johannes Crosigk von Pearson commands," the tall man said, and the children repeated his words. "And to never desert the service of the Republic."

Felix's mouth repeated the words and sat down with the other children after the tall man motioned with his hand. The man then paced around the room, shouting out phrases that the children dutifully repeated. When a boy with a stutter at the front of the room failed to replicate the words exactly, he stood up and kept his eyes on the ground as he approached the front of the room. The boy held out his wrists, and the tall man slapped them with a slender whip. The strike echoed through the air. With tears in his eyes, the boy tried again to repeat the phrase correctly but stuttered again. Again, his wrists were slapped. When he failed to reproduce the words yet again, he fell forward, his tears dripping onto the floor. The tall man stood over him with a grin. The boy pleaded with the tall man, but his wrists were whipped all the same; only this time, the tall man added a second strike for disrupting.

Despite his urge to move, Felix's legs were stiff in horror. He looked about the faces of the other boys in the room. A war ignited in Felix's chest: a want to help the whimpering boy at the front of the room fought against the thought of joining him. After a brief battle, the latter emerged triumphant, and Felix's body remained unmoved. He wondered after a moment if the same internal struggle occupied the other boys' minds. When he saw the other boys, they looked as terrified as he was.

The beaten boy slowly stood to his feet and sat back down. When the teacher resumed, the boy held his silence. Felix's eyes caught the teacher glancing over the stuttering boy with a faint grin and a glint of satisfaction at the corner of his face.

Even as he left the building, he held the image of the crying boy for the remainder of the day. The events he stepped through — as a passenger of his own feet — seemed like a place just over the horizon of the flat plains that he had passed through long ago but had forgotten during his time on the road. He walked along familiar streets, and knew that he was returning home after a day of school — the words seemed like abstract ideas that had lost their tactile meaning long ago. As familiar as the sands and the green mountains were, they were also alienating — they were so far away and so wrested from his mind that he felt like a foreigner. Felix's body walked through the streets, but he wasn't in himself as it did — he was in the mind of a young boy who had perished long ago in a place that no longer existed.

Felix's legs continued down the bustling street, passing through a slurry of familiar faces with no names. His legs sat down, and a one-eyed man dressed in rags approached him. Felix looked away, and the man went to another of the faces in the street.

"Excuse me," he said. "Do you have any money to spare?"

A few coins were tossed toward the one-eyed man, who fell to his knees to pick them up. Felix's head turned toward the one-eyed man as he hopped away. He was tempted to chase after the one-eyed man, but Felix's feet walked in the opposite direction, too afraid to go near him as he disappeared into the street.

Felix's body arrived home after a few turns and winds through a street. He wouldn't have been able to navigate had he been there without the pull of whatever force pushed his body forward. He recognized the small, ramshackle hovel at the end of the street — he knew instantly when his feet had arrived at their destination. A woman emerged from the front door of the house and motioned for him to enter. His feet rushed inside, and he sat down at a table in front of a pitcher of water.

The woman poured a glass and asked what sounded like a

question. Before Felix realized what the woman had said, his mouth responded and gave an answer he could not understand. The woman laughed and put a gentle hand on Felix's head. She said some more words that Felix couldn't understand, then she left the room. Her words sounded as though they had once belonged on Felix's lips but were now gibberish to his ear.

For the first time since he had fallen down the hole, Felix saw his face. His eyes peered into the water before him, and a face stared back — it was young, but he recognized it as his own. The face even included the long hair that had hung from his head for as long as he could remember. It was the first time that he considered the hair on his head. Part of him assumed that it had grown during his time on the road and was shocked to see that it had always been there. His neck stayed tilted down and maintained the sight of his reflection. The boy in the water looked lost and afraid — two emotions Felix had forbidden his heart from acknowledging since walking down the flat plains.

His body sat in silence as the sun shone from the window. Felix wondered what had scared the small boy he used to be — the tall man with the whip seemed the obvious answer, but the boy in the water seemed scared of something yet to present itself in the distant streets of the city. His legs stood up and walked into a room near the back of the house. His body collapsed onto the bed. As the loose straw of the mattress scratched his back, he felt his mind slowly fade into sleep.

* * *

The dirt suddenly gave way, and he fell into a cavern. The hole sealed shut above his head, sending a small deposit of soil tumbling down over his head as he landed on the large body of the man with the loud voice. He stumbled over himself, but also the man lying motionless. Felix tried to shake him awake, regretting his decision as the man's eyes peeled open.

"Whatever you think you're playing at," the man with the loud voice seethed, blood pooling from the top of his head as his eyes glowed with fury, "it's best you stop fooling around before you make me do something we'll both come to regret. I'm taking you back to the empire if I have to break every bone in your body."

Felix shook him away and jumped back, falling onto rough ground of the caverns behind him. The man with the loud voice stumbled after him but fell in a heap under the weight of his wounds. When Felix could stand once more, he ran into the depths of the caverns — no matter how far he went, the glowing eye of the man with the loud voice would always find him.

Finally, when he was out of breath, Felix had left the man with the loud voice behind in the caverns and bought himself some more time.

It was silent. The faint dripping of water and the breath of the mists sounded in the distance. Felix walked about the depths, trying in vain to find a path to the surface. He scratched his head considering how to climb back to the forest and return to the plains. He hoped that if he could find an entrance to the surface, even some distance from his original direction, he might find an unorthodox path to the forest. The great trouble was that he couldn't remember where he had been going above. When he tried to remember, all that came to mind was the image of the beast's horrible face and then a sudden flash of the horrors he had fled from in the town — of Cuthbert lying lifeless in the blood-stained streets.

Felix jumped back, having imagined that the ground had been shifting under his feet. Dismissing this notion, Felix kept walking only to jump back again as the ground shifted — sustaining its movement this time. He fell on his backside and watched the rocks creep into a long snake of stone that stood before him. The snake slithered near him, waving from side to side as she looked down and began to speak.

"What is this but some long-lost drifter trapped beneath the husk of the earth?" the snake asked as she looked over Felix's terrified expression. "What a pitiful thing these soils have brought me on this day. Such a broken, sad man you are."

Felix looked up at the great snake of stone. No eyes looked back on the rock face that hovered above him. He looked first to the floor and then to the snake, gathering his words as he struggled to speak.

"Please," he said, "I am only lost. I have found refuge, but I have lost my path. I meant no trespass. I was only fleeing from that horrible thing above. There's also a man — he's chasing me too. He tried to side with that horrible monster, and the monster pushed him down anyway — it carelessly tossed him into the pit where I fell. It was as though it didn't care if he lived or died."

"The blond beast," the snake said, nearly cutting Felix off. "A new, loathsome fixture along with the woods that wrought him. I can't tell you anything about that strange man following you — but I am too familiar with the blond beast.

"Once, he was a man like any other. Before he was the blond beast, his name was Albert Gould — an ordinary name for an ordinary man. He lived in a farmhouse and worked hard until his father failed to pay his debts. When his father was chased from the town, Albert moved in. There, he adopted their ways until he couldn't exist beside people anymore. As the days went by, Albert Gould died. A disease burrowed itself into his head and killed him, leaving only the base desires the town had breathed into his core. He lured seven men and eight women to their deaths so he could sell their organs. At his trial, he said that he was merely making a living. Then, the Republic removed him and planted some trees to contain what he had become. Shortly afterward, he lost the ability to speak at all. The Republic, of course, hid his true nature and spins pitiful tales that paint him as an elevated genius. They lie about his father and his acts — those fifteen people he killed have been effectively erased. Legend from beyond the woods says that he wanders the perimeter of the forest to find a messenger post so he can sell the organs of his victims to the highest bidders of the Republic once more."

Felix's thoughts turned to Doufsanctville & Avaramck as he listened, thankful that he didn't join the monster in the forest. It wasn't hard to see how a man like Albert Gould might emerge from such actions.

"More and more people from surrounding towns are starting to act like him — like animals mindlessly hunting for the meaningless spoils of pyrrhic victories. They dispose of their dead, their sick, and their injured in the woods — and they call themselves and that rapacious beast noble and magnificent for doing these terrible things. The poor fools — they can't see that their beloved beast will kill them too if it gets the chance. They don't understand that there was no danger here before they brought him into the world. They tell stories about Albert Gould being a hero, but Albert Gould has been dead for a very long time."

She looked closer into Felix's eyes. "But you are not one of them, I see."

Felix shook his head, remembering the beast's horrible face. The snake began to leave, beckoning him to follow. He stood up and trailed behind, his feet shaking with frightened anticipation as he walked.

The snake led Felix to a chasm at what he assumed to be the centre of the underground. She remained silent, slithering only in cold, swaying strides that echoed across the caverns. He watched the lines of the walls move and dance as he walked by, only for them to be still when he stopped to catch his breath. The lines spoke of a time long forgotten when they had been carved to service weary travellers who fell into the depths.

The chasm was an oval that curved away from the path, clearly carved into the rock by careful, deliberate hands. When the stone serpent escaped from view, the lines on the wall were all that kept him from being swallowed by the dark of the underground.

Felix turned a final corner, and sunlight poured from above onto the surface of the placid pond that rested at its centre. Felix entered the burrow, observing the detail, his one eyebrow raised. Into the rock, the lines that had led the way before flowed into images that covered the entire wall so that only mere centimetres of the original rock remained at a time. They showed a series of hands that reached above toward the sky as a herd of horned creatures ran before them. Felix squinted to see a tall, thin figure chasing the horned creatures and brandishing what appeared to be a knife. He nodded his head as he looked it over, slowly understanding its meaning.

"The blond beast is as impulsive as he is dangerous," the stone serpent explained. "You will never escape him as long as he shakes you. When you fear like an animal about to be eaten, you cannot use your wits. I will show you how to use your fear to outsmart that horrible beast so you can finally go forward."

"I can't," Felix said, shuddering as he looked over the carvings. "Surely there must be some way around that place. We're underground. Take me below until we are past the boundaries of the woods."

"Those are no ordinary woods. Run, climb — do as you like — but they will only grow and grow across the plains. Those trees were never meant to grow here. It took very strong energy to place them. That energy is a lot greater than you. Yet you can remain here, I suppose. But you will never reach your destination if you don't face the blond beast."

Felix shook his head and trembled. He looked at his hands — they were thin and shaking. He knew he was no match for the blond beast, but as he shook, he realized that the serpent was right — or, at least, that she knew better than he did.

The serpent turned toward him. She lowered her head and looked upwards. He saw a small, green light glow — the serpent's eyes had opened to see him.

"Fine," Felix relented. "Tell me what I must do."

The water on the pond rippled, sending waves over its surface. The serpent turned and slithered toward the water. Felix followed and looked into his reflection. A small school of fish swam about under the surface, darting away from the ripple of the tide — even they didn't know the origin of the movement.

The serpent turned to Felix but said nothing. He turned to her a moment and turned back to the water. A small breath was heard, and from the depths, a cup emerged and was carried to Felix's hand by the waves. It was a goblet of stone not found in the rock of the caverns. It held the reflection of the sun in a grip that refused to relent even as his hands turned the goblet to observe its entirety. It was fashioned in a way that pricked his fingers from unknown points as he held it.

"I can't remember who I am, but I know I'm not a good person," he said, looking at the surface of the goblet. "For as long as I can remember, I've been selfish and cowardly. I've just kept running. Now, my friend and an entire town have died for that. I can't keep being this way."

The snake coiled in front of him. "Then hurry up and drink the water."

Felix nodded. He drank the water from the goblet. When he swallowed, there was nothing but a cool sensation left behind. The serpent watched with interest as he stumbled backward, his eyes closing to the hum of the chasm. His shaking hands formed fists that released and reformed several times as he continued to topple backwards.

When his back met the wall, his eyes shot open. A tear of gleaming velvet fell to the earth, and he saw the air breathing around him. When he looked at his hand, he saw each pore and hair appear as it came into view. He saw the years of lines formed in his face, and he knew at once how old they were — he remembered being an infant and closing his hand for the first time. When he looked up, he could see each fold and curve of the earth — he saw around the rocks where they didn't meet and even made out a faint glimmer of sunlight when he squinted. He could feel every drop of blood in his veins. His eyes settled, and he saw the history of every stone of the serpent as she approached him.

"This is the sight," she explained. "It is a gift from this pond. Those who drink it see everything before them — from every crevice in every stone of the cave to every mite and every worm that dwells in it. In time, you will see visions of your past as they are also a substance of the physical world. But this alone is not enough to outsmart the blond beast. I must give you the knowledge that such a monster of arrogance and greed is too stubborn to consider."

Felix nodded as his eyes adjusted to his vision. As his eyes blurred in and out of the caverns around him, he turned — his eyes darted a great distance to the man with the loud voice. Even as his eyes flooded with images of crevices and climbing insects along the walls, he could make out a shaking scene. His head throbbed with pain as he watched but he couldn't force himself to look away.

He laid still in a heap but slowly rolled onto his back. Felix felt his heart racing as the man slowly regained his breath and stood to his feet. The man stumbled mindlessly in one direction, his hand on his hilt as he walked. Knowing that the man with the loud voice was moving assured Felix he was still coming for him, sooner or later.

The man walked with a fiery hatred in his eye — it burned with every stride of his mindless march. His hands never left his sword, and he licked his lips as he keenly searched for any sign of Felix in the caverns. Felix watched from this safe distance, wondering if his capture was truly the only thing on the man's mind.

The fear in Felix heart was mixed with pity as his eyes remained fixed on the distant remnants of the deposit that tumbled onto the floor of the caverns.

"Who is he?" the serpent asked suddenly.

"He's been following me for a while," Felix replied, trailing off. "He wants to arrest me for some crime, and he's willing to do anything to catch me. I saw him massacre an entire town. He's very dangerous."

"So why not hand yourself in?" the serpent asked suddenly.

"I can't," Felix replied, his sudden shudder at the thought confusing him. "I just — I can't."

The stone serpent said nothing as they kept walking. Felix turned back to the depths of the cavern as the man with the loud voice wandered forward once more. He would brandish his sword in anticipation at every rustle, only to sheath it as he found nothing. As he walked, he slowed his step and rested on the side of the cavern walls to catch his breath and nurse his wounds.

Felix could only turn away and hope that the glowing eye was as far away as it appeared.

FIXING THE WELL

HE FOLLOWED THE SNAKE deep into the caverns. As they descended, a deep green glow filled the air. Felix didn't dare to ask where they were going, even as a feeling of neither excitement nor fear sang from his chest.

The lines in the wall gave way to a new tunnel, which guided them toward a flowing stream.

Where water might be expected, Felix saw only green mist. The serpent stopped and commanded him to wait. He stood still as a flat log billowed over the mist and stopped beside them. The stone serpent crept aboard, and Felix followed.

"We are riding the flow of energy," the stone serpent explained. "No one carved this tunnel. It arrived as you see it and was made by the energy we ride over now. This is the same energy that flows through each of us, and it will take us as far as we must go."

Felix nodded and looked into the mist. The contrails danced like a fire, moving up and above the surface, adhering to the cycle of the stream. The green that burned within its essence was the same green glow that burned in the serpent's eyes.

As he stared deep into the depths of the mist, he saw each particle darting around its surroundings to give the contrails their motion. He sat, staring at the bewildering sight until his head started to sting with a pain that begged he stop his peering. His mind had still not caught up to his sight — he saw everything but understood little.

His head darted back — suddenly and against his will — to the man with the loud voice who continued to wonder mindlessly in the depths of the caverns, stabbing an insect with his knife and dropping it into his mouth. He was still far from Felix, but he neared the chasm. As his focus — inadvertent as it was — found the man, it burned a new pain into Felix's head, then his eyes.

He rested — the darkness of his eyelids seemed the only escape from the sensory onslaught — except he saw even more than with his eyes open. He saw the same energy flowing through his mind and the contrails of his thoughts billowing in the maroon darkness.

He opened his eyes with a sigh.

"How do I stop seeing all this?" Felix asked, turning to the snake.

The serpent said nothing, but her silence spoke loudly to his irritation. There was nothing more inescapable than that which lay before his vision. He thought about sleeping but knew that he would only dream of these particles and the green mist he now understood to be everywhere.

From the midst of his vision — as if to interrupt his irked state — a small number of spires emerged. They were buildings, standing a small distance from the log as the mist pushed it gently. Felix winced, setting his eyes upon the buildings and finding them to be dwellings of some sort.

"A village of crows," the stone serpent said, answering his question before he spoke. "They observe you above and then cackle below at their findings. We will see what they have to tell you, given that this is what the mist commands."

Felix nodded. He had no say in the matter, but appearing as though he agreed helped to quell his feeling of helplessness — until he became aware of it. Then, he could only feel eager to leave the man with the loud voice behind in the caverns.

The log arrived at the shores, gently shoving itself onto the soil island that lay in the middle of the mist stream. Two crows hopped over, a look of taciturn judgment churning quietly behind their eyes as they looked upon Felix. He could see their hearts beating and the green mist moving their feet as they walked, but their thoughts remained hidden from him still.

They came upon the shore, looking upon Felix and the stone serpent beside him. With a shared caw of reluctance, they turned and waited for them to catch up. The crows walked quickly, their wings flapping occasionally in a manner that suggested a temptation to fly. Felix struggled to keep up with them, even on foot. The stone serpent simply continued moving, paying no mind at all to his faltering breaths even when he felt his heart pounding in his throat.

"We know why you're here," said one of the crows. "I am Gwan and this is my wife, Mitto. The mist never let us down before. But why a man of all things? And this grim figure following you around — an odd companion to bring to these caverns. Who is he?"

Felix tried to explain only to fall over his words, having described the man with the loud voice so often that it now sounded absurd. Mitto snickered to her wife in a caw that met like a cackle in Felix's ears. These were the first words the crows had said since they had begun to walk toward the spires of their village. He was tempted to respond, but admitting he didn't know what they were talking about seemed a risk too great to take. Gwan's comment only brought Cuthbert to mind.

Felix fought to stop himself from getting lost in guilt.

The ecru soil they walked on was damp with the mist from the stream. The cavern persisted still, save for a few small holes above that allowed for faint glimpses of sunlight to trickle down. Where the light hit, small greens sprouted from the soil. Young crows nipped at the leaves while some adults flew in from above, carrying building materials, foods and trinkets in delicately woven baskets. Others stood chattering in the street or tending to the quotidian business of repairing the various buildings. Felix walked through the scene, watching every particle of it unfold. He rubbed his temple as it began to strain from observing every contrail of energy held by every crow in the village while he walked through.

The other crow turned back to look at him. Felix was sweating from the sights around him — sights he couldn't escape. He looked up to the bird, straining with pain.

"Do you know why we mock you?" Mitto said with pity. "We mock you because of what you do above. At once you are pitiable — you men. You stumble about, and without the comfort of your glass and your plastic, you would surely die. But that isn't it. The pigeons shared your tragic story. Because of what you did to them, we don't just laugh because you are amusing — we also laugh because we are angry and we do not understand you."

Felix grunted and sat down. The crows surrounded him, the anger in their eyes turning to confusion. The stone serpent stood between them in silence.

"What happened to the pigeons?" Felix asked, sitting on the ground. "I don't understand what you mean."

"Then you must be told," said Gwan. "Those birds helped you to deliver messages in times passed. They were your allies, and you had no quarrel. But you gave up on them when your loud, mumbling metal things came around to do the work for them. Then, you let them loose in the cities and left them to grow fat on the pieces of bread you threw to them. And now, you meet all together to figure out a way to be rid of them. You created them, you disposed of them, and now you want them to disappear because they remind you of your own shortcomings — I assume — and yet you still hold yourselves as above us — you men."

Felix looked up through the pain at the crow above him. When a tear came from his eye, he did not know if it was from the saddening tale or from the searing pain in his brow. Then he thought carefully — the first consideration he made since he had received the sight — and he knew that the tear carried both origins.

"He doesn't know, but he understands," the stone serpent explained, looking carefully upon the two crows as she spoke. "That is why the mist sent him. He is one of many men like that — a touch above those who know but don't understand and those who are satisfied being bereft of both knowledge and understanding. There is hope for him and for others like him. Unlike most of them — unlike the loud one trudging aimlessly about in the caverns — he wants to change."

The crows nodded, looking upon Felix more carefully. He could see the confusion leaving their eyes. In its place, there stood a hesitant hope that grew stronger as Felix stood up.

"Come," said Gwan, "we have a task for you, Felix."

He nodded, wiping the tear from his eye. He couldn't remember telling them that name. Mitto and Gwan took him to the centre of their town. There stood a mangled collection of frayed rocks covered in dust. The mess of ashen decay spoke of a towering monument that had fallen in times gone by.

"This was once our well," Gwan explained as Mitto nodded her words into Felix's memory. "We had a system to convert the green mists into water. Yesterday, we found it broken like this, and now you are here. I'm not sure if this is a mere coincidence, but you must help us, please, try to repair our well as best as you can. It is clear that you have the sight. This can only be done by one who carries it."

"I will," Felix said, looking over the disarray of rocks.

The crows gave a final look of faith before they departed back to the village to help with the repair of a hut. Felix watched them alternate between tending to a pair of crow chicks in a little nest at the base of the hut and hammering various nails into the wood where it had grown loose. A smile crept across his face.

"I can't help you," the serpent said, and he turned to face her. "I can only watch. If you're to learn to use the sight, you must do this task alone."

Without another word, Felix turned to the rocks. He set about walking around them to see where they had been prior to the fall. He wanted to observe the various cracks and blemishes that covered the strewn remnants. The other fixtures in his vision darted before his eyes in a manner that stopped him from seeing anything else. He circled the area, attempting to find a simpler starting point before he knew how to repair the entire well.

As he walked, he learned to use the sight to find what he was searching for. It was a laborious task that carried much pain. Felix stood, clutching his head in frustration as he searched desperately for the place where the mist had become water. He sat and strained until his nose had grown bloody, before he saw it — unobstructed by the other fixtures of particles, contrails and their links that persisted in his vision. When he saw the meeting place at last — the bubble foam that quashed mist into water — he felt himself grinning.

He fell to the ground and closed his eyes. This time, he saw only the particles of darkness that nearly quelled him into a sleep. He had command of his eyes again, and his head hurt no more. With an instinctive squint, Felix turned back to the caverns behind him. He only caught a glimpse of the man with the loud voice before he decided to turn back to that which lay ahead of him.

Felix stood up and looked over the rocks again, finding their rockfalls in relation to the bubble foam; the knowledge came to him. The rocks soon showed their cracks and he knew where to place them. He was a small man, but he understood where to push a rock larger than him so that it stood upright. There were five rocks that required this beside several more that needed to be brought back to their place.

He pushed the five to their original shape, manoeuvring around the moss and the weeds that grew on their sides so that no extra damage was done. As he worked, Felix could fit the rocks in a tight, sturdy formation. He watched each of their sides as he moved them carefully. His arms were strained, but he allowed the weight of the rocks' motion to carry the majority of the work. He was a mere guide. Time passed like the flow of the mist — neither rapid nor prolonged — and soon the well was granted shape again. When the five were in place, he filled the gaps with the remaining smaller, loose stones.

He stood back and looked at the newly formed well before him. Felix grinned as he saw the bubble foam quashing the mist into water and filling the cylinder above, only to stop in horror as water began escaping through the remaining cracks. He felt a twinge of embarrassment for missing the leaks which only turned to panic.

He ran toward the village, searching frantically for some sort of adhesive to stop the oncoming flood suggested by the relentless flow of the water. His eyes fell upon some crows placing bricks upon a wall. Felix explained himself, and the crows quickly nodded thanking him for repairing the well and handing him a bucket full of concrete liquid with a trowel.

Felix knelt by the well, patching leaks as the serpent watched him carefully. He felt his breath give way again, but he kept covering the leaks until the water stopped pouring. Only then did he finally rest. Though he could see that the bubble foam functioned properly and that each leak had been patched, he walked toward the well with a feeling of concern in his heart. Felix took his hand and ran it gently through the water. His heart finally calmed its beating as he felt the water continuing to flow gently.

With a deep breath, Felix turned back to the caverns — the well had distracted him from the man with the loud voice for long enough. He found him again, wandering aimlessly in the depths of the caves, but his glowing eye was now dangerously close to the village. He turned to the crows as he saw the man getting closer.

The serpent approached him, swaying from side to side in strides that told Felix she was pleased. She stopped beside him and turned to the well, only to stop with an air of concern as she followed his glance.

"You did a good thing," she said. "Now, let us hope that this time the well holds." Felix nodded.

"He's getting closer," he said plainly.

The serpent darted forward and turned back.

"It's that man who was following you, isn't it?" she asked.

"He's dangerous. He massacred an entire town in front of me

— and he killed my friend."

The stone serpent coiled back toward the village as the glowing eye of the man with the loud voice pierced through the air. The man with the loud voice unsheathed his blade. The serpent let out a hiss — a sound that resembled two rocks grating against each other — and a flock of crows screeched as they descended upon him.

"Gussie!" the man cried out, swatting hectically as the birds evaded his slashes — with only one eye, his aim had worsened significantly.

Felix ducked for cover, knowing that he would be useless in the fight as he watched the birds effortlessly evade the man's blade until he lost balance under the onslaught of the crows and the blood loss from his wounds. With a thud, he fell into the stream and drifted away.

The two crows that had greeted him turned away from the scene of the attack and landed before the well. They sipped from it and turned to him. All that remained churning in their eyes now was gratitude that neither crow tried to hide from Felix's sight.

"Thank you for this," Mitto said, her voice darkened by the shock of the attack. Felix looked to the stone serpent and then to the crows.

"Who was that man?" Gwan asked after a silence. "Not one of Jalopy's men?"

"No," replied the stone serpent, "I doubt that."

"He's here for me," Felix said, turning away. "I'm sorry, I've put you all in grave danger."

"That stream will carry him away," Mitto said, turning to where the man had fallen.

"I am sorry for asking," Felix said, rushing to change the subject, "but I must know — what destroyed the well?"

Mitto and Gwan shuddered to respond.

"We have only a small notion of this — nothing more," Mitto said. "But those of us in the village believe that this was the work of the man known as King Tarragon Windsor Jalopy. He lives north of the great curve in the stream. He and his armies have been trying for some time to take our village — perhaps he thought that sabotaging our well would weaken us enough to ease his conquest. This is the only explanation that anyone seems to be convinced by. We've had this well longer than anyone can remember, and it has never broken before. King Jalopy comes and three days later, this well is shattered."

Felix sat down again. He focused his attention on the stream. It flowed on longer than he could follow it, but there was a curve that he found immediately. Ahead, a great castle stood. He watched soldiers marching in the open courtyard as a king stared down upon them from an opulent tower.

When he looked back to the village, he understood what he had to do. Mitto and Gwan nodded toward him. The serpent led him back to the log in the stream. As they stood, they watched the log get swallowed by the mist below.

"We don't need this anymore," said the serpent, preparing to enter the stream. "Stay close to me, and we will avoid drifting away into the current."

Gwan and Mitto looked at each other.

"We want to carry you," Gwan said, "but we can only take you so far before King Jalopy tries to shoot us from the sky."

Felix nodded and the snake came away from the stream. "Thank you," the serpent said. "We will do what we can."

The crows took them and soared just above the roof of the cave. They carried Felix and the stone serpent until the curve became visible. With a shared nod, the crows released their grip.

Felix looked up to see Mitto and Gwan flying away as he plummeted. When he landed in the water, he struggled to keep himself above the surface. He searched desperately for the stone serpent. Only when she came to push him toward the castle in the distance did he grow calm once more.

Felix looked into the mists and watched the waves curl back into the streets of his home. He tried to look away, but his eyes were drawn to the image in the mists — it was the only thing unaffected by the sight the snake had given him.

He sank back into the young boy's shoes, but this time, the distant streets felt slightly closer than they had at first. With the feeling of walking through the streets slowly returning, Felix saw a more familiar sight — the sight of the town as he left it for the first time. He saw an image slightly closer than the young streets of his childhood. He sat in a dark room with only a small beam of blinding light running through it and a feeling that he had to escape as soon as possible.

He had run away — that is what sent him down the road for the first time and, ultimately, where he was now. He looked up from the mist for a moment and kept walking in the caverns. The sight sent the small crevices of the ceiling dancing back into his eyes. The resulting migraine made him sigh and he turned his vision back to the mist.

* * *

He returned to the young boy he once was. His feet once again moved on their own and took Felix to the school as usual. The tall man emerged, and his name returned to Felix — he was Maro Wergil, the teacher at the school. Mr. Wergil peered down from his high shoulders with a grin that sickened Felix's stomach. As his feet took their place, Felix felt a twinge of fear wash over his spine. Mr. Wergil entered, and once more, the sound of the oath of loyalty echoed through the room.

The boy who had led Felix's feet to the school sat behind the stuttering boy. They shared the name Ephraim, meaning that they were known among the other boys as 'Stuttering Ephraim' and 'Tardy Ephraim' — Mr. Wergil always used their surnames. Felix's mouth finished the oath, and his legs sat down. As his body moved, his eyes glanced at Stuttering Ephraim's wrists — they were still bright red from what Felix could tell. This vision must not have been long since the previous one. Mr. Wergil stood in front of the class and waited until the entire room grew silent.

"Today," he said, "we will work on your reading skills. As Mr. Tibber showed us all yesterday, several of you still struggle to speak in a manner befitting the children of the greatest empire in history. I shall pass this great poem around and each of you will read it aloud. Remember, this is the glory of the empire you hold in your hands."

Mr. Wergil opened a book and handed it to a boy on the far end of the classroom. Most of the boys were able to read the poem — a short recounting of a battle — without fail. When an initial failure was made, Mr. Wergil cracked the whip on the offender's knee. Only when the book reached Stuttering Ephraim did the punishment escalate. He struggled with the middle line of the poem, and his first stumble was met with the expected strike on the knee — but Stuttering Ephraim soon followed it with a second, and the whip struck his arm. After a few more strikes from the whip, Stuttering Ephraim made his way through the poem, holding back his tears as Wergil moved on.

Soon, the book made its way to Felix's hands. Felix's lips tried to read the words but soon reached a strange word he mispronounced. He felt the whip against his knee and his mouth tried again. With the second mistake, the whip thwacked against his arm. Felix expected a full beating to be administered when the sound of laughter made him hesitate. Felix's head turned and Mr. Wergil put his hands on his hips — Tardy Ephraim sat snickering in his seat.

"Don't waste your time, sir," Tardy Ephraim said. "That barbarian won't get it right. It's like expecting a dog to tell you our entire history. That's simply not his nature."

Before Mr. Wergil could reply, Felix felt his arms lift him from his seat. His legs propelled him forward into Tardy Ephraim. His body pinned the boy on the ground, and his fists were launched over and over again into the boy's face with a heavy impact that resounded through the floor. With every strike, Felix wondered why the other boys let the scene play out and why Mr. Wergil didn't intervene. When Felix's body was finally out of breath, Tardy Ephraim's face was covered in bruises — his nose bled and his jaw was covered in deep sores that left lines of red all over his face. His legs stood up and left the beaten boy to hold his face. As the other boys glanced over Felix with terror in their eyes, he felt a wave of guilt wash over him both as the young boy he once was and as the young man he had become.

It wasn't this incident that made the empire banish him to the darkness of the room, however. Mr. Wergil marched over to Tardy Ephraim as he lay on the ground and lifted him to his feet. With a knowing glance, Mr. Wergil left the room and returned alone a moment later. He finished with the book and moved on to the next lesson topic. The words Mr. Wergil spoke from that point forward were unclear to Felix as the guilt screamed loudly in his head. When school concluded, his legs stood up, and he returned home.

Again, the same woman appeared and poured another glass of water. The woman said some more words that Felix didn't understand and left again for the back of the room. A large man emerged through the door — Felix's hands began to shake at his entrance. He sat beside Felix, and it became clear that the large man was his father.

"I heard about your fight today," he said. "Whoever it was probably deserved it. Don't worry too much. Now you've shown you're a man. I don't think any of those little boys will bother you again."

Despite the words of his father, the feeling of guilt didn't leave Felix — in both the past and the present, it only grew stronger. The large man struck Felix's back with a light touch of pride before leaving. Now, Felix understood why the boy in the reflection of the glass looked so afraid. The large man stood up and the table shook with his step — he found the woman at the back of the room and she looked away from him, her eyes finding Felix as he sat at the table.

His mouth had no more words to say, so his legs stood up and went back to the bed.

Felix expected to leave the room and return to the mists, but when the darkness left his eyes, he saw nothing past the sun of early morning. When his legs took him to school, Felix saw an empty stool where Tardy Ephraim used to sit. His eyes stared at it for the remainder of the day, even as Felix wanted his head to turn away.

* * *

He suddenly felt his head give way and his eyes were filled with darkness — when Felix felt control of his arms once more, he had already returned to the mists. Up ahead, he saw the man with the loud voice being carried by the current. He rubbed his eyes as he watched a few soldiers — though their uniforms didn't belong to the legion — fish out the man with the loud voice, throw him to the ground and draw their weapons as he crawled forward.

He blinked the vision away and focused on moving forward.

They swam desperately through the green fog. Felix felt his arms grow tired even as the stone serpent continued moving her tail through the limitless flow of energy. When he looked into the waves, he saw the contrails falter as they neared the shores of the castle. As they approached, the contrails suddenly darted away and returned to the remainder of the stream. The result was a loose wall of energy that left the floor of the stream bare as it ran beside the shores. By the time they approached the floor, he was able to walk toward the castle that stood abruptly in the distance of the caverns.

Felix readied himself for what was to come.

KING OF NOTHING

FELIX LOOKED UP — the soldiers had turned, seeing the stone serpent slithering along the bare floor of the stream.

"Stop!" a voice called, pulling Felix into the moment, and he felt a pair of arms take him from the stream and toss him carelessly onto the ground as the stone serpent disappeared back into the depths. "State your name and your business on the shores of the great King Jalopy."

Felix answered immediately with his name but began to struggle as he thought of his business. The glances of suspicion from the soldiers told him that if he lied, they would know. He looked first to their boots, then back to their eyes.

"I am here on behalf of the crow village," he explained, instantly regretting his choice of words. "My business is to inquire as to the origins of a recent attack on their well and to request that King Jalopy cease his conquest of their lands at once and withdraw from these caverns."

A soldier responded with a strike from the butt of his rifle that knocked Felix unconscious.

* * *

When he awoke, he found himself being dragged into the cell of a dungeon. With a smirk, the soldier who had struck him locked the door.

Felix slumped to the ground, wondering what to do next. He clutched the sides of his head, gritting his teeth. Then, he heard the sound of clapping bounce from the bars of the cell. He turned to see an old crow in the cell, clapping her feet together as she looked into the light that flooded through the window. She saw him, and she approached slowly.

"Well," she cawed, glancing over him, "this is a strange sight. Normally, I don't see humans in this cell. It's always crows or some other bird that those soldiers catch. I flew too close to their shores when I returned from gathering straw for my village. They took the straw, and they forgot about me in here. So, human, what did you do to end up in this cell?"

"I told them to leave these caverns and to explain why they attacked the well in the crow village."

"Ah yes, only a human would be so arrogant. As long as his children sleep, King Jalopy won't stop blaming everyone he sees."

"His children?"

The crow laughed and went back to clapping her feet together. Felix sighed as he looked about the cell. He saw the way the lock fit together — its various hinges and components were easy to see through the keyhole — he just needed to find something small and sturdy enough to pick it. He searched the cell, combed between the stonework and found a wooden twig just sturdy enough to crack at least this one lock. The twig was filthy and faded from the sun — the guardsmen must have missed it in their cell sweeps for months, and it became a fixture of the room. He brushed off its muck, then whittled it against a sharp stone corner before pushing it through the components of the lock until it popped open. The crow looked up, watching the cell hang wide.

"Aren't you going to leave?" she asked when Felix stood still, staring at her.

"It's not for me — it's for you," he explained. "I just arrived, but if they've forgotten you, they won't know if you're gone. You can go home now."

The crow laughed again, but she leapt toward the open iron door. She looked at him with a smirk in her beak.

"I keep doing things just for myself — it's time I did something for someone else. Go, please. I promise I'll do what I can about the king."

"You're arrogant to think you can solve everything wrong with these caverns, boy." She hopped out of the cell as Felix opened the door. "That won't get you very far — especially not with one eye pointed forward and another looking endlessly back. But I am grateful to you for this."

Felix nodded, and the crow ran to a window and flew off into the sky. He worried that she might be caught, but there were no signs of panic as she left for the skies. He could only hope that she would make it back to the village as she disappeared into the horizon.

* * *

He felt a small part of him slip away into loneliness as he slumped onto the floor, wishing he hadn't opened the door to the cell. Felix sighed, letting the thought leave with his exhale as he settled into his situation.

The still stone walls of the prison cell danced before Felix's eyes in a frolic of dynamic grain. He held his knees to his chest and rocked gently from side to side as a deep searing overwhelm poured into his head.

His eye was soon caught by a small piece of dust that lay precariously in a groove on one of the bricks on the wall across the prison cell. So many other specks of dust had fallen into the spaces between the bricks — this one speck resisted the pull of gravity. Before, he would never see such things — even without the sight, the rebellious speck of dust was plain to see with a slight squint. As Felix watched the speck, he slowly began to imagine what the wall felt like from where it stood. He closed his eyes, watching the veins in his eyelids as he imagined it falling to the floor at last.

When the speck hit the floor, he was back in the dark room and the blinding light shone into his eyes once more. He squinted into it, but all he could see was a white void that burned his vision as he stared into it. He turned to see where the light ended, but the sight was gone — he couldn't see its end. Felix crawled about in the brightness, searching for a wall. He made half a step only to stop for fear of discovering that the room was smaller than he had imagined. As he stopped, the blinding light was blocked, and a voice sounded.

"Who do you think you are?" the voice demanded.

Before he could respond, the room disappeared, and Felix found himself on the streets of his childhood. He realized that he was crawling on the pavement — he stood to his feet but froze in shock as he realized that his legs were his own this time. He turned his head and saw the bustling street — his vision, he too had control over. Felix thought it strange that none of the passing faces glanced in his direction but decided that it was because they had other things on their minds. As he walked, he realized that he was slowly making his way to school.

The other schoolboys marched into the classroom. Felix joined them with a small rush in his step as Mr. Wergil rang the bell once more. As Felix approached, he noticed that all the seats were taken, save for the stool where Tardy Ephraim sat — he looked to his own place and saw the terrified young boy from the water glass. He looked at his feet and saw that they were as far from his eyes as usual. No one in the room looked at him or asked why he stood in the hallway. Felix grit his teeth and saw Mr. Wergil standing just beside him — his eyes were on the class and unconcerned with the strange man in the doorway who bore a strange resemblance to the timid boy near the window. Felix swung his hand in the air, levelling it toward Mr. Wergil's face — when he expected his hand to make contact with the teacher's face, it phased harmlessly through his head and sent a cold shiver up Felix's arm. Mr. Wergil kept speaking as though Felix were not present at all. He stood back and helplessly watched as the lesson continued. The children recited the oath and Wergil began with more phrases.

"I believe in the one and only Lord, the Father almighty, maker of heaven and earth and of all things seen and all things unseen," Mr. Wergil said and the children each repeated.

Stuttering Ephraim remained silent and sat shaking in his chair. Mr. Wergil left him alone and continued with another phrase. Felix watched the young boy near the back of the room glance at Stuttering Ephraim with a twinge of sympathy — he remained seated and repeated the coming phrases as best as he could.

When the day ended, the terrified young boy stood up and went in the opposite direction of the flowing sea of schoolboys rushing home. Felix followed him, slowly recognizing his path as they continued. The young boy descended a staircase into a dark basement — no one was in sight, and it appeared as though no one had been for some time. The boy walked down the steps with a confidence that suggested he had been to the basement before and a sense of caution that suggested that he knew the area was off-limits to school children.

At the foot of the staircase, there was a door with a single window on top of it. The basement was bright with fluorescent lights that hummed in Felix's ears as he passed. The boy looked through the window on the door, extending his height by standing on his toes. He held the image for a time, staring blankly with an expression that conveyed no emotion.

Felix stood behind the boy and saw a room padded with white upholstery that stung his eyes as he saw it — he wondered how the boy could stare so long. In the centre of the room, a body lay in a heap, breathing frantically. The body moved and its head raised into the light, revealing the face of Tardy Ephraim — he had dark circles beneath his eyes, his clothes were drenched in sweat and his skin was covered in abscesses. The boy stood still, watching Tardy Ephraim for several seconds.

Felix called to the boy desperately, telling him to help Tardy Ephraim to escape. When no reply came, Felix started to wonder why he felt so frantic. He stood back, defeated as the boy continued to stare before swiftly turning and leaving the basement.

Felix went to the cell and tried to open the door — his hand phased through the handle and the cell remained locked. He glanced again at the boy in the middle of the room. He felt guilt return to his chest as he realized that there was nothing he could do. A short while later, Mr. Wergil went downstairs and opened the cell with a key.

"Ephraim Romley," he said, shaking his head. "You are constantly late and now you go and provoke a savage. If I didn't know any better, I would say that you were among the least gifted in the classroom — the future does not look well for you. Ah well, come on out. I hope a night's rest in the company of our Lord has done you some good."

Wergil opened the door and picked up Tardy Ephraim by his neck. He pushed his back and told him to leave. When Tardy Ephraim didn't move, the teacher shook his head and turned to walk out.

Tardy Ephraim waited until Wergil was turned away from him towards the door before grabbing the teacher's legs and pulling him sharply, his front losing balance and toppling to the ground. Wergil's head struck the edge of the thick cell door on the way down. The teacher lay motionless on the floor as a pool of blood formed around his facedown skull. Felix approached him, his mouth hanging open — Wergil was still breathing but could only twitch his sweating fingers.

Felix stood back in shock and Tardy Ephraim fell to his knees crying. A man came down the stairs and demanded Tardy Ephraim what had happened.

"He fell," he sobbed. "He was climbing the ladder and he fell."

The man frowned and threw Tardy Ephraim to the floor in the cell without a second thought. He carried Wergil's limp body out of the cell as he kicked the door closed. Felix ran toward the door, trying to prop it open — again, his hands phased uselessly through as the door slammed shut. Tardy Ephraim threw himself against the padded walls and yelled loudly as the man abandoned him in the basement. When Tardy Ephraim grew quiet, Felix looked to see if the teachers would return, and when he looked back, there was only darkness.

The voice repeated its question, "who do you think you are?" He opened his mouth to respond, only to fall short of words. He felt his throat — when he tried to speak, it remained unmoved and free of vibrations. The voice laughed and Felix lunged forward toward the place where the blinding light had been.

* * *

Felix struck his head against the bars of the cell. He grunted in pain, nursing his head — once more his throat resonated with sound. Footsteps echoed through the halls. As the steps grew louder, he stood up and closed the door after removing the whittled twig from the lock. Soldiers marched through the dungeon room doors.

"King Jalopy will see you now," nne of the soldiers said. "Explain yourself briefly and clearly and you might be released."

Felix nodded as they unlocked the cell door. He followed the guards out of the dungeons and into a narrow hallway. They travelled up a winding stairwell through to an ornate hall. Columns as wide as tree trunks supported the great hall's arched ceilings high above their heads. The walls were each adorned with tapestries of armour-clad knights who stood, waving weapons above inscriptions of their past conquests. Felix stared up in awe as he was led to a series of stairs that sat below a massive, gilded door. Guards standing on either side of the stairs stood at attention as Felix was led through the doors into the throne room.

King Jalopy, the ruler Felix had seen atop the tower when he arrived, sat on his throne, dwarfed by the massive oil portraits and the tall arch of the chamber, resting his head in his hands. With a wave of the king's hand, the soldiers left the room.

"My council has spoken about you — all day we've been conversing about the mysterious men that have emerged in these caverns. You aren't from these parts clearly, so they're all of the opinion that you must be a spy for the crows," King Jalopy said, approaching Felix to observe him closely. "But a spy wouldn't be so foolish, so brazen as to tell me to leave."

Felix looked around the room and then stared into the king's eyes. He was no different from any other human being — his organs, his bones and his muscles all functioned in a manner consistent with anyone else. He stepped toward King Jalopy.

"Why do you want these caverns for yourself, anyway?" Felix asked, stopping himself from being intimidated.

King Jalopy was taken aback by the confident tone in Felix's voice. But then, he responded with a grin that spilled into his grey beard as he revealed his teeth.

"I'm searching for a cure," he said. "My three children fell ill the day we arrived here to take the land for the kingdom. They have all drifted into a sleep they cannot be awoken from. I commanded my peasants to work as fast as they could to grow every herb in search of a cure, but nothing would cease their slumber. I searched everywhere here for some sort of medicine to wake them up again. Then I heard that the land home is infertile now. All the peasants have turned to rebellion. Now, there isn't a kingdom for me to return to. In our absence, those peasant rebellions were crushed by that wretched empire, and now they've absorbed everything. We can't go to war with them — we have nothing. I tried to have their emperor assassinated, but alas, we couldn't finish the job. If anything, it's only strengthened that fool in the eyes of the public. My children — the future of their people — have fallen ill with a wicked illness that has even ruined our country's crops. I have no choice but to do this, you see."

The king's grin formed into a sombre scowl, his voice lowered in sorrow. "I just wanted to hear my children's voices again. But why would a common man care about the politics of my dominion and my family? I shouldn't bore you with the details."

King Jalopy waved his arm in anger. Beyond a sheer curtain across the room, he could see them — three children — two boys and a girl — in carefully polished stone beds. They were each arranged so that their arms rested by their sides, their hands lay on their stomach and each of them was covered by a thin white sheet. Felix extended his sight through the space between the sheet and their heads to see their faces. None of them looked older than fourteen. He returned focus to the king, trying to let the sympathy he felt in his heart show itself on his face.

"I'm sorry," he said, a compassion burrowing into his chest. "But you can't take the crows' land. They have nothing to do with your children's illness."

"Oh, but haven't they?" King Jalopy seethed through his teeth. "My father wanted these caverns too once. They chased him away. And on his deathbed, he made me promise to take it for the kingdom. This must be some sort of tactic. They are hoping I'll return home and give up — that I'll yield. But I'm not giving into those pathetic little birds. Not now, not ever. I will destroy every part of their little village until they relent, and they release my children. It's a battle of wills, you see."

King Jalopy smirked and settled his voice to his original neutral tone. With a motion of his hand, a servant boy came through the chamber doors and promptly poured him a drink.

"So you did destroy that fountain," Felix said, walking closer to the throne. "You're lucky no one died. It didn't work on the empire, why would it work on the crows?"

"That's war. The crows may not understand the concept, but that's what this is," King Jalopy replied, nursing the glass with loose fingers. "We're both trying to win, so I can't begrudge them my losses, nor can I pity them for my victories. I'm assured that they will fight back, and I honour their efforts, but the fact is that they will lose eventually. It's an ugly thing, but in the end, what will come of it will be far more beautiful than what came before. Had I been successful in toppling the emperor, I would say the same for him. Do you think I like this? Do you think I want to be sitting here festering in these childish games?"

"You're pointlessly taking innocent lives," Felix said, feeling anger in his voice. He felt an outrage that was foreign to him and a connection to the crows that he couldn't understand.

"Maybe getting rid of the crows will solve nothing, but when they're gone, we'll be able to search the remains of their village for a cure. My people come first. They always have."

"Those crows have done nothing but live here without ever harming you. They have had nothing to do with your children — I doubt they're even aware of it," Felix said, his voice nearly reaching a yell. "You have no right to plunder everything they have in the feigned hope that they might find a cure to your children's illness. That's pure insanity."

King Jalopy motioned for the servant to leave.

"And who are you to question my presence here, boy? Where would I go? What would you do if you were sitting on this throne with tens of thousands of people at your feet, asking you to lead them? What leader in history hasn't sought to plunder the earth for the good of his people?"

Felix said nothing, the anger in him burning out any words. He was tempted to grab King Jalopy and throw him from the window if it meant that he wouldn't be able to hurt the crows any longer. He stepped back, realizing that this would do nothing.

Time passed slowly in the throne room. The flames of a nearby torch waved at a laggard pace and the king's eyes followed. As Felix looked at the children, he saw the past once more — it poured in through the window and beckoned him to enter. At a loss in the throne room, Felix approached.

* * *

When he walked into the streets again, he suddenly felt the gravel of the road under his feet. The eyes of passing faces glanced at him now — he was himself and he was in the time he saw. Still, he felt the winds of the past pushing him in a certain direction as his mind became two men — one in the past on the streets of his childhood home and one in the present, standing blankly in the throne room of King Jalopy.

Even as he re-experienced the past as himself, it was still impossible to change anything. He recalled his words and his actions — they moved with a will that had once been his but that had since left him behind. The dark room seemed closer than ever — even as it remained absent it felt as though it was looming just beyond the images that danced before his memory.

The day was bright without warmth, and he remembered that this day was only a short time before he had started to walk the plains. He had awoken one day in Dagastay — one of the largest cities in the Republic — and walked to the church in search of a job. His parents had grown old, and they had no money to support his education at the Vasta Academy for Boys. His mother began to teach him on her own, but as she grew old, she had difficulty remembering what had been taught. It was a well-known fact that the church held a special status in the city with benefits that were difficult to turn away. So, he approached and asked the priest about a position in the clergy.

He had been going to the church for some time now. When he went to church, he was sure to sing the hymns louder than anyone in his row and to memorize the words in his spare time — he stayed long after the service ended to clean up the pews. Bearing his special efforts in mind, the priest looked over him.

"Ah yes," he said, "I remember you — you were one of Maro Wergil's students. He was a great donor to the church, you know. If you are ready to devote every moment of your life to the service of our Lord in heaven, then you are welcome to join us as an understudy."

"I am," he replied eagerly. "I can think of no duty that would be so full of meaning and purpose."

"I am glad," the priest said with a look of slight surprise. "But there is yet one concern left," he tried to hide his anxiety as the priest spoke. "You see, what your mother has named you is a coo — a sweet noise akin to the gibberish of infants but unbecoming of a grown man, let alone a servant of the Lord. That isn't a name at all. Now, so you are to serve our order, you will have the gift of a name. August shall be your name as long as you serve under the Lord and we are your family, and so, as my son, you will carry my name. You are now August Orosius."

August nodded, accepting the name.

"Welcome to our church, then, August," Father Orosius nodded with a grin and took August inside, washing seven years by as he walked.

The time of those years was filled with empty, disjointed moments that swept past Felix's mind as August walked into the church. The church gifted a spacious new house to August's parents where they lived happily into their old age. August saw them less and less as he continued to work in the church. He prepared for countless sermons and services, but only a single sermon remained intact in Felix's memory.

"We are not animals!" Father Orosius said during the service. "We are endowed with the reason of the Lord — He created this world for us alone."

The details of the sermon escaped Felix. He could recall only the words of the priest and the visceral reaction of disgust he had upon hearing them. Despite his disgust, however, August still shouted in agreement at the conclusion of the sermon.

Then, the fateful day arrived for Felix — Father Orosius approached August with a sorrowful look in his eyes.

"I'm sorry, August," he said. "But I come to you in this holy place with terrible news unbefitting of the altar. Come with me to my office so I may impart it to you."

With a concealed sigh, August followed Father Orosius into his small office near the back of the church. They sat at tables, and over a pot of fresh tea, the priest began.

"There is no easy way to say this, I'm afraid. Early yesterday morning, both of your parents were found dead in their home of causes yet to be revealed to us. I can only assume that the Lord took them for their age and that he keeps them. May they rest in peace."

August nodded and rested his head in his hands. Tears never did come — his resolve to the parish fortified his emotions, believing his parents were now safe in the Lord's hands as Father Orosius said. When he went home, his parents had already been moved to the morgue and he was alone in the house. What surprised August was the surreal comfort he found in the silence of the house as he sat alone in the living room. August remembered that the church had made him promise that if he had more than he required, he should give it to the poor — he ignored the thought and napped on the couch. During his sleep, a week washed by, and Felix he couldn't recall anyone ever confronting him about the house.

Still, this was not the crime that had put him in the dark room — when the day of the funeral came, August was still living alone in the house. The man with the loud voice hadn't started chasing him yet.

* * *

Felix blinked and the flame in the burning torch sped to its typical pace once more. He looked over his shoulder, searching for any trace of the man with the loud voice as he faded back into his thoughts, only to shake his head back into the throne room. Felix clenched and released his fists as he looked into the king's eyes — they watched him blankly, holding his image at a distance with no intention of approaching. The children lay still under the sheets, moving only to breathe. Felix stepped toward the curtain.

"This audience has been a waste of time," King Jalopy said. "Guards, take the prisoner away."

He motioned for the soldiers to return, but Felix raised his hand as he looked carefully at the minds of the children — they were troubled and throbbing in their skulls.

"Wait," he begged. "Please, let me help your children."

Felix turned to King Jalopy. His stunned expression soon turned to anger again. He motioned for the soldiers to enter again.

"This insolence has only sealed your fate," King Jalopy spat, turning to the soldiers. "Take the prisoner away and prepare the grounds for execution. I want this filthy little crow spy shot." A soldier saluted and dragged Felix back into the dungeons. The cell door slammed shut and he frantically searched his mind for something he could do about the coming annihilation of the crows. The anger swelled into defeat as he fell to his knees.

Felix took the twig from the ground again when the soldiers had gone. He opened the lock again and crept toward the window. He thought about running down the steps, but then he realized that guards would be nearby. He stared out of the window, wishing that he had a pair of wings instead of the sight which only seemed to make him see every inch of the looming destruction.

Below the tower, a busy market continued. Soldiers — tired and weary — stood over the crowd. Felix wondered how many of them knew that the crows were innocent and that they held a market little different from this — only in the crow market, no one sat alone.

He looked about until he found a small door that led to an unseen backstreet. Felix crept to the door, keeping an eye on the soldiers from behind a wall until it was safe to slip out. Keeping his head down, he ran toward the stream of mist.

* * *

After a short while, the stone serpent emerged again. She approached Felix and stopped just before his nose. He could only look to the ground in shame and disappointment, knowing he did little to convince the King of anything.

They entered the mists, and she led him toward the village as he explained the situation. "Why did you tell the king to withdraw from the caverns? That isn't what you were sent to do," the serpent asked when Felix had concluded.

"That's what we want, isn't it?" Felix said, feeling his voice grow defensive. "If he leaves, he won't hurt the crows anymore."

"He can stay in the opinion of the crows," the serpent said. "But he can't remain as he is." Felix furrowed his brow.

"Come," said the serpent, "I'll take you back to the village, and you will learn more of how the crows wish to resolve their conflict with King Jalopy."

As they climbed onto the shores of the village, a small crowd of crows formed. Each of them had questions that were spoken rapidly and atop one another at a rate that Felix couldn't hope to hear — let alone understand — amid angered calls decrying his decision to speak on behalf of the crows and call for King Jalopy to leave when he was an outsider. When the crowd died down and everyone could be heard, he realized that many of the things that he could have said had been told to the village already by the crow from the dungeons.

"I know how we can send him back, though. His children are bound to some sort of sleep. He blames you crows, and he is hoping that the war will make you leave."

The crows laughed. Gwan and Mitto came forward.

"It doesn't matter," said Gwan. "Even if his children woke up, he would still attack us. Don't take us for fools. Whatever happened to them is just a way to make his people believe in this fight. There have been many of that family who have tried to take these caverns before. They have lost each time, so now this new King Jalopy wishes to take away our strength and then take our village when we are too weak to fight back. That is why he destroyed the fountain. The children have little to do with it."

"Perhaps," replied Mitto, "but we should at least try this idea. The human is arrogant to think that we can change the mind of this king by awaking his children — let alone to speak on our behalf and tell him to leave — but I can see no other means of ending his violence.

Perhaps the event can awaken reason in him, and he will finally cease. And if this doesn't happen, we will have helped his children. I can see no reason not to at least attempt to resolve the conflict."

Another approached — the crow Felix had released — and stopped just before his nose.

"I am Equill," she said. "I am grateful that you released me and remained in the dungeon yourself. That demonstrates that you will go far, but you still have much to learn. I offer you my best wishes. I will fly above Gwan and Mitto to show them the best route with which to deliver you. With my route, you will not be detected even as you land."

The other crows backed away from Equill and turned to Felix as they did. Equill looked back at the village and turned back to Felix with a look in her eyes that begged for a reply.

"Thank you," Felix replied. "But I must be caught for this to work. It is the best way into the tower."

"As you wish, Felix," Equill said, turning toward the crowd. "But if you require my services, I will be watching. It is an honourable thing to try to do this, but what a stupid thing it would be for you to die for."

The crows murmured in slow agreement. Felix stood back, listening. A strange part of him considered taking the children captive and commanding King Jalopy to leave. His stomach churned at the thought — this is the tactic of the empire, of this kingdom. What good would it bring if he were to succeed? He considered the potential of more violence being brought to the crows in retribution for these acts, so he decided against suggesting it.

He turned to the stone serpent, who appeared disappointed in him even through her stone face. It was decided that Felix had to return to the shores of the kingdom and attempt to awaken the children since he had suggested it — despite his return to the tower, he put himself in danger again of execution. This was a risk Felix was willing to take.

Gwan and Mitto flew him and dropped him as near to the shore as they could where he was met by the same squadron of soldiers. Just as quickly as he had escaped, he was locked again in the dungeons, awaiting execution once more.

IMPRISONMENT

HE SAT IN THE CELL, his fate shimmering over his mind as the light dappled through the window. The twig he had used only a few hours ago to escape was still on the ground where he had left it, and he could still see that the broken components on the lock he had picked were only crudely repaired. Felix held the twig in his fingers and twisted it around. He was tempted to flee again, but something stopped him now that he had escaped only to return.

Through a small gap in the mortar between the bricks, he saw a tall wooden post being hammered into the ground before eight riflemen. They fired all at once, shattering the post as King Jalopy emerged to complement their aim. Felix thought about being executed — about standing before those riflemen and defiantly warning them to leave. He would die, but he would be remembered. He would lie in the ground, but the crows would always remember him.

Then, his mind turned to his wandering on the flat plains. His wandering there and his confusion seemed so small now. As he had traversed the barren landscape with nothing but a name to call his own, he had been walking above the drama that now engulfed his entire existence. At that time, he didn't even think about the ground beneath him or what may lie beneath it — only his next destination.

His thoughts stopped suddenly at Cuthbert. He hadn't thought of him in some time and a feeling that he should have kept his friend closer in his mind caught him off guard. He had insisted on staying

— on avoiding the task he had been given — and now Cuthbert was dead. Felix looked at his filthy boots, scanning the bits of dirt that had been lodged deep into the seams as he wondered if he had listened to the old woman, perhaps Cuthbert would still be alive.

If he hadn't insisted on going to Doufsanctville & Avaramck instead of searching the forest like the old woman suggested, maybe Cuthbert would have never gone to Doufsie. Maybe he wouldn't be meeting his fate alone. Maybe Cuthbert would still be alive. Maybe the people of Doufsie would be too.

* * *

Felix began wandering again through his sight. His escape from the dungeon cell had been a challenging endeavour itself. Now, he seemingly was trapped in the darkness, with only the voice and the blinding light for company. Sometimes, the light would be blocked, and a plate of slop would descend before him. Eating the slop only made him feel hungrier, but Felix feared what may happen if he let his body starve.

He lived through a shapeless cloud of time that merged minutes into what felt like years. On a whim, he took some of the slop in his hand and threw it toward the blinding light. He tried to explain to himself what he was doing, but he couldn't. He heard a small squishing noise as the slop fell onto the floor in front of the room and a pattering of footsteps rushed to meet it.

"What are you doing?" the voice boomed as a banging on the door sounded. "Do you want to starve? Is that what you want, Gussie?"

"Wouldn't you like to know?" he responded, the words escaping his mouth. "You must be an idiot if you haven't figured it out. What an idiot you are! I have never heard anyone so stupid as you. You can't even figure out this one simple puzzle, you idiot."

Without warning, he began to rock from side to side and a strange feeling boiled in him — he could only think of a singular word to sing out as loudly as he could.

"Idiot! Idiot! Idiot! Idiot! Idiot! Idiot!" his voice bounced about wildly in the darkness as he puffed the word out of his diaphragm in a hoarse pseudo-melody.

The voice grumbled, and suddenly the blinding light flooded the cell and a tall shadow stood above him, carrying a club. Without thinking, he ducked through the shadow and let the club strike the remaining darkness. As he ran forward, he felt his eyes burn to see in the light. A pair of shoes behind him turned on their heels and he ran as fast as he could toward a door — the first thing he could see clearly — in the hopes that it wasn't locked. The door gave way, and he tumbled down a hill and into a rainstorm. When he landed in a heap at the foot of the hill, he laughed with joy and looked up at the hill to see a great dark building atop it.

"Idiot!" he cried again between his laughter.

Slowly, his laughter died down and he realized that he had to run. He charged forward through the rain and kept his feet pounding forward until he reached a long, abandoned gravel road. With his hands in his pockets, he trudged forward until the rain stopped and revealed the empty flat plains. Then, he walked endlessly forward in search of a location that was never apparent, even as these memories played out in his mind once more.

"Idiot," he said again. "Idiot, idiot, idiot. Such an idiot."

And he repeated the word until he couldn't remember anything else.

* * *

Felix blinked again and looked about the cell. All was quiet.

He turned his head and stared at the light pouring from one of the windows. At least this time he could be locked away in a prison that wasn't shrouded in darkness. He put his head on his knees and watched a small ant, crawling along the floor until it found a small hole in the wall — just barely big enough for its body — and disappeared.

He felt himself beginning to call out to the ant, but he stopped himself, afraid he was losing his mind. He shook his head and closed his eyes for a moment. He yawned, feeling his limbs grow heavy.

Slowly, a shape emerged from the corner of his eye. The man with the loud voice sat, propped up against a wall in the cell beside him, his face twisted into a grin. He shook his head.

"Well," he said through his teeth, "isn't this something? You're right where I want you — in a cell facing a firing squad — but under the wrong authority. These bloody halfwits can't see the value in an alliance with the empire, taking me for some sort of spy, so here I am too. Not to be executed, though. They want information from me. It gives me time to decide if I should give their location to the empire, or maybe we can share some reward for the execution of August Orosius."

"Such an idiot … " Felix said again, peering through the bars as his memories danced and weaved in his mind — his words made the man with the loud voice straighten up. "Jalopy is the one who tried to kill your emperor, and you expect him to help you? Why don't you try arresting him? Go on, try it. I'm sure you'll get double the reward."

"First I — we — have to get out of here. Help me apprehend the king and maybe they'll absolve you. You could be a hero."

"You expect me to fall for that?" Felix replied holding in his laughter. "You really haven't changed at all." He stood up and started pacing as the man with the loud voice furrowed his brow, his grin fading. "I can't remember everything, but it's coming back. All that time you kept me in that room, did you ever think you'd learn what it's like to be locked up?"

"So you are him," the man with the loud voice said. "Well, that'll make the empire happy."

"You're like a flea, you know," Felix spat sharply. "Every time I stop thinking about you, you worm your way right back into my head; every time I turn around, there you are. Why can't you just leave me alone? Why do you follow me like this? Why did you kill all those people? What, for justice? For the empire? For a beast who pushed you down here right beside me?"

"He was helping me," the man with the loud voice retorted. "He was putting me ahead of you. We serve the same purpose. I should be so lucky to be half the man Albert Gould is."

"How many lies do you have to tell yourself before you realize you're being cheated? They're using you. Do you think that the empire would care at all if you died right here?"

"Well, why should I care if they don't? I have accepted my duty, and I will do whatever is necessary to see it fulfilled. If I stick around long enough, if I apprehend the most hated people in the empire — the failed assassin who tried to kill our emperor and the profane heretic who disgraced our church — I'll be the most respected soldier in the legion. Just think of what I could do for justice — for civilization — in such a role. If I die in the attempt, I'll be a symbol just as valued. A martyr, even."

"You would lay down your life alongside countless others in the name of this so-called duty?" Felix seethed, hearing the venom in his voice. "Never once, not even at my lowest, did I let myself turn into that kind of scum. You're not just selfish, you're something else — something much worse."

"What would you know, Gussie?" the man with the loud voice spat back, his words still echoing off the walls even under his gruff monotone.

"That is not my name!" Felix spat back, taking a step closer and hitting his face on the bars of the cell.

The man with the loud voice smirked as a guard entered. "Ready to talk?" the guard interrupted.

"Sure," the man with the loud voice replied, standing up. "But it'll likely be more of the same. You really should consider my offer and what the empire can do for you."

The guard rolled her eyes and opened the door, pushing the man with the loud voice down a hallway. Felix sat down again, turning his head to the side. He held his head in his hands, letting his heart calm itself from his outrage. He felt his eyes grow heavy as he sat in the cell, letting the seconds pass through the air.

Before Felix realized it, he had already fallen asleep.

* * *

August woke up on the day of the funeral. The ants in his house had become such a nuisance that he placed small pieces of honey-coated paper on the floor in the hopes that they would become stuck to it. So far, only a single ant had made the mistake of approaching the paper and word of the traps had quickly spread among its companions. In the end, the paper was nothing more than a waste of good honey.

With a sigh, August picked up the bits of paper and tossed them into the garbage. He poured himself some coffee for breakfast and sat down to prepare his eulogy for later that afternoon. As he reviewed the words, he felt distant from them and a growing part of him pondered the point of the eulogy, the funeral, and soon afterwards, the church. August finished his coffee and stood up, ready to go for a walk to clear his mind before the service.

When he left his house to lap around the streets, August was met by the sound of a pleading voice. He turned to see Habil Bartimous — a poor man who could often be seen panhandling in the streets — blinking through his only eye. Rumour had it that Habil had sold his missing eye for a single piece of gold which he then gambled away. August simply didn't know, given that Habil had been on the street for as long as he could remember. To his memory, Habil only ever had one eye, but the story seemed probable to him.

"Please sir," he said, "I'm poor and I'm hungry — won't you spare a small coin so that I might eat tonight?"

August ignored Habil and walked down the street. Habil rushed toward him and August turned around. Habil pleaded silently with a sympathetic smile. August looked to the ground before turning away and leaving Habil in the street. As he turned, he felt an air of jealousy breathe into his lungs — Habil Bartimous, the poorest man in the city, was happier than August had ever been in his life. The man with nothing, who found joy in gambling and drinking — vices the church forbade August from pursuing — was soaked in happiness. By simply asking passers-by for a little money in a polite, measured voice, Habil could acquire anything he needed throughout the day — August had to speak nonsense in the church just for a meagre salary and a modest house for his dead parents.

He kept walking, alone in the crowded city until the time for the service finally arrived. With each step, he wondered more about the point of living.

August found himself at the pulpit of the church, flanked by his parents' coffins. The small crowd in front of him were comprised of faces he couldn't recognize apart from the priests — Father Orosius sat in the front row with a sorrowful expression. With a deep breath, August began with the opening hymns. Faster than he could remember, the sermon concluded, and it was time to deliver his eulogy.

"We are gathered here today to remember the lives of my parents," August began, shifting his weight between his feet. He saw the remaining words on the page he had written but struggled to speak them clearly. "They were there for me when I was young, I know that much for certain but when I try to remember them in detail, there's nothing. I hear only gibberish when I should hear their voices. It's not surprising, I suppose. I'd left to study, devoted my life and work for this parish, and it's been at least seven years since I last saw them for any real length of time. Now, they're lying here, and I don't remember a thing.

"The last thing I remember is my father congratulating me for beating a boy into a pulp. I don't know where that child I struck is now — only that the last time I saw him, he was in a cell under the school. I was glad about it because my father told me that I stood up to him and he got what he deserved. He never spoke to me like that before, and his words confused me — or at least, they did until today.

"The last time I spoke properly to my mother, she said words I couldn't understand and called me a name I don't remember. Since then, we'd been like strangers living in the same house. And that's all because I thought learning to speak like you would bring me good things in this world.

"I started to think like you, to talk like you and to act like you because if I was going to survive next to you, I had to become you as much as possible. My father thought that — when I beat that boy nearly to death, he knew that's what you expected of me. Is that why no one ever told me that it was wrong?

"In reality, I am nothing like you and I can only see it now because instead of burying my parents, I am burying two strangers. So, what do I have now? A house? A congregation telling lies? A spirituality foreign to my way of being? I have nothing left! You — all of you, the Republic, the church, the empire — you took everything from me! You ripped my tongue from my mouth before I was even born."

He struck the pulpit with his fist as he spoke, and a deafening silence filled the pews of the church. August caught his breath in the cathedral's silence. Slowly, he led the crowd in a final prayer before exiting, leaving the people at the funeral and the bodies of his parents behind.

On his way back home, Father Orosius caught up to August and stopped him.

"August," he said. "If I am to speak candidly, you have made a mockery of the church and you have desecrated it as a place of worship. Not to mention, you could very well be executed for your treasonous words against the emperor and the Republic. Were I not a man of reason, I could mistake you for a dissident and a barbarian rebel — you are lucky that my better senses tell me that your parents' passing has clouded your good judgment. Take a long rest from your duties and pray for forgiveness and for the souls of your departed parents. In a fortnight, I will consider allowing you back into the order."

Father Orosius dismissed August with a wave of his hand. He continued to his house, his eyes turned to the road in shame. He opened his door and fell on his bed, suddenly bursting into laughter. When he saw the cross looming above him, he tore it from the wall and threw into onto the ground — he couldn't remember when it had gotten there, only what it now represented. He laughed again until he ran out of breath, and he lay, unable to sleep on the bed. He remained there, staring at the fallen cross through the night until the light of the sun poured once more onto the streets.

August stood up to walk the streets. As he went, he felt an emptiness devour his chest that didn't leave until Habil emerged.

"Sir," he said again, "please, could you spare a small amount of money — just enough so I can eat. Please, sir, I hate to trouble you, but I haven't eaten in four days, and before that, I had only a small loaf of stale bread. Even stale loaves of bread are a rare find for me, you understand. I'll do anything you ask just for a small morsel of food."

August ignored him once more, even as he followed him up the street. As Habil's voice grew louder, August tried to hurry his step, persistent in his pleas, until August felt himself turn and strike him across the face. As Habil fell to the ground, August leaned over him with a blank stare.

"I'm sorry! I'm sorry!" Habil cried, crawling away. "Please sir, let me leave. Please forgive me. I won't bother you any longer. I meant no harm." The pleas only made August step closer and kick Habil in the chin repeatedly until he stopped moving.

* * *

Felix jumped back. When he saw Habil's face, he saw Cuthbert staring back at him with cold, lifeless eyes. He felt him against his foot again and an urge to vomit crept into his stomach. He stood up and frantically paced about the cell, searching desperately for any sign of guards to release him from the past but he saw it all the same.

* * *

August left Habil lying motionless in the street and let out a wild staccato laugh. He then rushed about the street to find the early scramble of the market. With another bout of laughter, he began kicking stalls and throwing their contents into the streets.

"Father, why?" one of the merchants cried and August realized that he was still wearing his cassock.

"It's meaningless!" he replied. "There's no point to any of it!"

His rampage continued through the streets, leaving everything he saw in a wreck until his eyes fell upon a basket of fruit. He turned to see a pair of approaching legionaries at the far end of the decimated marketplace. August took the basket of apples and ran away with them, fleeing toward the outskirts of the city.

The legionaries chased him until he left the city's limits and ran along the farms of the countryside. When he was finally out of breath, August let out another laugh and looked at the basket of fruit he still carried. He turned to see a pen of pigs and emptied the fruit over the fence. He stood, watching the animals clamour to eat the fruit with a grin when a pair of gloved hands grabbed his shoulders. August turned to see the legionaries before him with a set of chains.

When the Republic put him on trial, Habil Bartimous wasn't ever mentioned — he couldn't even remember if he had died or not. The high priest, shaking his head mentioned only the theft of the fruit and the vandalism of the marketplace. As with all trials in Dagastay, his sentencing was left to a vote by the people. A silence hung over August as he looked into the eyes of the bewildered crowd.

"Hang the savage!" someone suddenly called, breaking the silence and the words were met with a thunderous applause.

The judge held out a hand and the crowd quieted down.

"I hereby sentence you, August Orosius, to languish in the prison under the charge of First Manipole Martin Scorpsnow. You shall remain rotting there until dead. Lord have mercy on your soul. Send him down."

The legionaries threw August into the dark room. The door

slammed and slowly, the walls of his new home faded into view. The chief legionnaire placed in charge took special joy in tormenting August through the small opening in the door where a sliver of blinding light shone through. His loud voice battered against the walls.

CHILDREN

FELIX BLINKED AS THE SUN PEERED into his eye. He stood up and realized that he had now been in prison three times. He chuckled to himself until he decided that it was better to be executed for something he believed in than left to rot in a cell. As he kept pondering over it, he wondered if the reason he kept being locked up was because he had done so many things that had gone unacknowledged.

A tapping sounded on the window and the present returned. Felix turned to see Equill standing at the window.

"Hurry up," she said. "We need to get you out of here. I don't care what they said in the village. I think it would be stupid for you to die like this."

He shook his head.

"They'll kill you, and that's the end of it."

"Maybe, but I can't just run away. I've been running too long. Maybe it's time I pay for what I've done."

"You're an odd little man, Felix," Equill turned sadly to the window. Felix reached out his hand and asked her to stay in the sky, should she be needed later. She ruffled her neck feathers, but she agreed to do as he asked.

Silence returned to the cell as Equill flew from the barred window. He thought of the woods and of the terrifying thing that lay within them — that horrible blond beast with its ferocious strength.

As the image of the woods returned to his mind in vivid detail,

Felix picked the lock again. After little effort, he was free.

He looked about the tower, searching desperately for the throne room. The halls were empty, save for the occasional guard. Each of them had a look of apathy on their faces. As Felix crouched behind flowerpots or pressed himself against the corners of dark hallways, he was tempted to imagine that his superior skills were what kept him from view. The realization that it was likely the apathy of the guards stuck in his chest as he crept closer to the throne room.

He arrived in the room, pushing the door open slowly. Though the guards of the castle were seemingly unconcerned with Felix's prowling, they would almost certainly rise to meet an intruder in the throne room for their own sake. Felix approached the curtain and looked through it to find the children still sleeping. He searched the room, squinting carefully for details missed since he last confronted King Jalopy.

He quickened his pace as he heard a door slam. He looked through the keyhole of the chamber doors to see a pair of guards searching frantically, heading up the flight of stairs towards him. Felix sprinted, crouching behind the throne as they entered.

"Would be a strange place to hide," one of them said. "If I were a prisoner, I'd escape. Why waste time sneaking around?"

"I just do what they tell me," the other replied.

They looked around the room with a routine, surveying glance before slamming the door shut and continuing the search elsewhere. Felix snuck back towards the door, squinting through the keyhole to ensure the great hall was unoccupied. As the guards continued their search for Felix, he turned back his attention to the children in the next room.

He pulled the room's curtain to find it bare of decoration, save for the sleeping children, their beds, and a weeping old woman next to them. He wandered closer to their beds. The old woman looked up; her face reddened with tears.

"They just lay there," she said, too sad to ask Felix who he was.

"I wonder if they will ever awake. It's like they're dead already." She started sobbing again as she went to each bed.

"Safil, Carba, Cevec — I still remember their laughter. When their mother left them, my duties increased. And now, their father has no one but himself."

She sobbed again. Instinctively, Felix approached her, with widened eyes and placed a hand of sympathy on her shoulder. She looked at his clothes.

"You aren't from this place," the old woman said. "But I can see your heart. It's beating with pity for these children. The crows won't get anything if you just stand there."

Felix felt his eyes twitch open with confusion.

"I have been watching this place for a long time," the old woman said, her face shifting as she looked into Felix's eyes. "These children are now having to play a part in a conflict that they are too young to know the stupidity of. Some say this is some unknown disease that has taken to them, but the only disease that is killing them is stubbornness and pride. It is all too common here."

Felix stood back and saw the old woman shift and morph before him. From her back, four tall, hairy legs sprouted as her arms and legs extended and narrowed to meet their shape. Her eyes divided into several brown irises as hair sprouted from her face and her mouth became a pair of jaws that clicked.

Before him, a spider twice his size stood. He stood in awe, unmoved by the sight before him. "Those above think I am some sort of pest — a danger, a carrier of poison. Many fear me and cannot say why," she said, climbing to the ceiling. "But this cannot stop me from my duty — I remain above their heads, where I catch their bad dreams and I help them sleep," Felix looked up. Above his head there was a large cobweb. Between the various strands, he saw cocoons wrapped around throbbing green energy.

"You see," the spider explained, "the mind creates good thoughts on its own, but worries, doubts, contempt and bad memories all come from surroundings. When the mind sleeps, it is at its most vulnerable, and so spiders must keep those thoughts from entering. The trouble is that this place is covered in destructive thoughts and these children cannot awake because they are too overwhelmed." She crawled back down. "No crow could do that."

Felix nodded.

"Can I see these dreams?" he asked. The spider looked up to her webs.

"Certainly," she said. "But these dreams are more turbulent than anything I have ever seen before. I have not been able to contain them and there are many more just as horrible that get caught in the web. I am but one spider — I cannot fight this alone."

"Neither can I," Felix said, the words falling from his mouth. He had learned to stop speaking without thinking, but as he said those words, he felt his heart pound with strength. It grew stronger as the spider looked at him with approval.

"I remember you, Felix. You've changed a lot," she said. "Not that you would remember me. We will attempt to do this together. You are but a small man, but I will gladly take any help I can find."

She told him to climb on her back and she leapt into the air and climbed up the cobweb. She took him to several cocoons and told him to take a handful of the green. Then they came back down, and she told him to put the green into his hair so that it would find his mind.

"Don't worry," she said. "This is not enough to make you sleep — it will only show you a small amount of the bad dreams."

Felix nodded. A pounding at the door sounded, to which the spider left Felix in the cobwebs and transformed back into an old woman and answered it. Over her shoulder he saw three guards.

"Just a routine check, madam," said the guard in the middle as they surveyed the room.

"No one here," the spider explained as the old woman. "Just me and the children."

"Well, alright then."

The guards left with a shrug. The spider let her disguise loose again and turned back to Felix. "That will buy us some time," she said. "The guards here are not interested enough to care about us for the time being. Most of them have been here too long to be anything but jaded. You really must hurry, though."

Felix nodded and he placed the green over his head and let the images fade into view. The visions he saw were different from the sight — he could no longer peer about to get a better view — there were no cracks or crevices to speak of. Instead, the image encompassed his entire view and only followed his eyes when he attempted to look away.

First, he saw the oldest. He stood in a room, flanked by a dozen advisors as he overlooked a map with tears in his eyes. Below him, the map was red. Felix looked closer to see that the map rested in a pool of blood that spilled into a gap on the table.

"My lord Safil," an advisor said, "what will you do? There is a rebellion in the west." "Well," said the young king, "can't we listen to them? Surely they aren't just rebelling for the sake of it."

"I must urge against it, sir," the advisor said. "If you give in now, then perhaps the entire countryside will turn against you. They'll bring violence to your kingdom as a way of getting what they want. We have to push them back now."

The young king cried, signing a document with a hand that struggled to move. He fell back into his chair as screams resounded in his ears.

The daughter followed. The altar of a wedding stood. The pews were filled with people with blank patches of skin where their faces might be found. They applauded periodically as she walked up the aisle. She stopped in front of the crowd and found a man with a crooked grin before her. He was several years older than her and he kept his hand on her shoulder even as his bony fingers wrapped around her wrist.

"Princess Carba," he said, "may I say what a great honour it is to take your hand in mine. I will make your father proud. I promise."

She forced a half-pursed smile onto her face as she agreed to marry him. The crowd applauded again, and the man put his cold hand onto her shoulder and guided her toward the exit of the church.

Finally, the younger son appeared. He sat in the throne room, overlooking the people below. He carried a face that suggested an apathy that matched that found in the guards. He began pacing throughout the room, glancing occasionally out of the window. His pacing took him to a dining room. He was alone at the great table, eating food that brought images of the starving people beyond the doors next to him. Servants bowed and left the room in a cue.

"We're at your service, my lord Cevec," they said as they finished their monotone introductions.

When he returned to his room, the young king was too tired to sleep. All he felt able to do was lay awake in his massive bed, knowing that he would never meet the people he was meant to represent. The world beyond his window was burning — the flames could be seen even from his view. The look on the young king's face spoke of a man who had grown up too quickly and had long since given up trying to argue with his advisors about stopping the fire. As Felix watched him, the striking loneliness echoed throughout the dim image even as it faded away.

One final image occurred. In it, Cevec and Safil stood, carrying spears and guns as Carba watched on. She looked away and her brothers covered their eyes as their feet carried them toward a crowd of shuddering crows. The clash brought blood and destruction into the air.

As the images disappeared, Felix returned to the throne room. The spider caught him as he stumbled over his lost balance. She eased him to his feet and scurried to face him. As she looked into his eyes, Felix thought of the images. He approached the children again, wondering desperately what he could do.

"I don't know how to help them," the spider sobbed. "Every day, there are more of these images, and they are held in their slumber. I want to take away the source of their pain, but the source is this place and the actions of their father. I'm not one to stop such things, at least, not without making things much worse."

He looked up at the cobweb and fell to the ground in defeat. As the children still slept, they appeared peaceful — a state that hid their internal torment from passive glances. Felix felt his head fall into his hands.

"We have to do something," he said.

The spider stood in saddened silence as Felix sat, pushed to the ground by the weight of the hopelessness that filled the room. He recalled what the spider had said. Then, he stood up and turned to the spider with the beginnings of a grin creasing his face.

"We should take them from here," he said. "Put them in the mists where none of these images are."

The spider shook her head. "I've tried such things before," she said. "This place is too heavily guarded. I'm just a spider — I have to crawl somewhere. There is no way I wouldn't be noticed even in the form of an old woman as I took these children from their father."

"But you aren't working alone anymore." Felix ran to the nearest window. Below, guards hurried about lethargically in search of him but — in their persistent apathy — never looking to the sky. He saw Equill flying above the town and he waved to her. She landed outside the window. The spider turned.

"Fly these children away," she said, approaching Equill quickly. "If you do this, they may be able to wake up again."

"What about you?" Equill asked, turning to Felix. "They'll kill you if you stay." Felix approached and looked to the floor.

"This isn't about me," he said, looking up to meet Equill's glance. "They might kill me, but if these children being awake will convince their father to end this conflict, then so be it. I can't act only for myself anymore. That will only make things worse."

Equill nodded and flew away with the children in hand, disappearing through the skies. The spider shook her head and climbed from the window. As she neared the ground below, she morphed into an old woman and joined with the crowd. Through the curtain veil, Felix saw King Jalopy marching into the room. The king was followed by the guards who had surveyed the throne room only moments before.

Felix turned to join them and threw out his hands, awaiting his fate. They bound him and King Jalopy struck him with a fist to the gut.

"You are the lowest assortment of bottom feeder on this earth," King Jalopy spat. "The sooner you are put to death, the sooner you will be unable to hurt anyone again."

The King turned to the empty beds behind him and kicked Felix to his knees, furrowing his brow as he fell to the ground in pain.

"But as a final act, you have made my children disappear. You cowardly, pathetic excuse for a man," he said, clasping Felix's chin with a tight grip. "I want you to know that when those guns remove you from this world, the crows will follow. They are not long for this world now."

INVOLUNTARY ARMISTICE

FELIX LOOKED TO THE FLOOR as they dragged him through the halls. For a moment, he worried about the danger he was putting the crow village in. He wanted to avoid this altogether and felt ashamed of his efforts. Only when he thought of the children awaking did he realize that he had accomplished something. He didn't care if he would be remembered or forgotten — he would live on among the grains of soil that danced before his eyes as he was dragged outside.

The guards fastened him to the post as drums sounded in the distance. He turned to find the man with the loud voice tied to a post beside him. The second post had clearly been hammered into the dirt in haste — the wood was shattered near the bottom.

"They weren't interested in that deal," the man explained suddenly, answering the unasked question. "Humiliating — dying like this."

"You get to go exactly as you intended," Felix replied with a grin. "You get to die for justice," the man with the loud voice fell quiet and looked to his shoes.

The squadron cleaned their rifles and saluted King Jalopy as he stood, glaring into Felix's eyes. He returned the look with an expression of acceptance — if he was to die, he would not be able to stop the bullets. The riflemen began to load and take aim as Equill, Gwan and Mitto descended upon the field, each carrying one of the children on their back. Soldiers ran into the field and took aim at the birds. King

Jalopy ran out, tears welling in his eyes as he realized that his children were awake once more.

"Don't shoot!" the king cried. "Those are my children!"

He stopped before the birds. "What is the meaning of this? Unhand my children at once."

"They awoke us," Carba said, climbing down to face her father, "by taking us away from this place. It was this war and suffering and our place in it all that put us to sleep."

Seeing the confused look on her father's face, she continued. "Throughout all of this — all this war, suffering and death — did you once consider us? I don't want to get married. My brothers don't want to command a nation. We don't want to be a part of this."

King Jalopy turned to Cevec and Safil who nodded in agreement with their sister's words. The king turned in confusion to Felix. He nodded.

"This place is what made them slumber," Felix said, raising his voice from his place on the post. "You did this, Jalopy."

"The crows had nothing to do with it," Mitto explained. "Now, please, we woke your children, and we brought them here. There is no reason that you can't live here with us as equals."

King Jalopy shook his head violently. "No," he said. "This is manipulation to get us to leave what is rightfully ours. Who do you crows think you are? You think you can blackmail your way to victory? You are too cowardly and weak to die with honour, so you fight with slime instead."

Carba stood in front of Equill. "We won't slumber again," she said. "We were trapped with horrid images of the future you have made for us. So, either you abandon this pointless conquest, or we live with the crows."

"How many people have to suffer until you see that you can't go on like this?" Felix shouted, finally finding his time to speak. "Look around you."

The guards, who had been nodding in agreement with Carba's

words. By chance of fate and her convincing words, they began to lay down their weapons.

"This man did more for your children than you have done for any of your people all your life. I won't die fighting a war that makes no sense against an enemy that has done us no harm," one of them said, and all other guards nodded in agreement. "Good luck fighting a war with no army. We don't need you. We never have. None of us have ever needed or wanted a king. The only reason you are here is because we feared your absence, even as we hated it. But now, it is clear that the crows have an alternative. They don't have a king, and they seem much happier."

"What is this?" the man with the loud voice shouted, suddenly emerging once more in Felix's thoughts. He swayed back and forth instead of gesturing as he stood tied to the post. "Are you all too stupid to understand that without a king, you'd all be at each other's throats? You could be such a great ally to the empire if only you handed over this fugitive. You could be rich. Your conflict could end. Is none of that important to you?"

Felix turned as a guard undid his bonds. He walked toward the man with the loud voice and knelt down to pick up a rifle from the ground. He had kept the man with the loud voice from his thoughts for so long as best as he could, but now he finally looked into his eyes. Loading the gun, Felix placed the barrel against the man's forehead.

He then remembered Cuthbert — and all the people of Doufsanctville & Avaramck. As he looked again into the man's eye, he saw his pupil quivering with terror — gritting his teeth, he finally understood.

"Martin — Martin Scorpsnow," he said, dropping the gun at his feet. "I'm not going back to the empire. You've been keeping that image in your mind for so long that you fooled yourself into believing it to be plausible — inevitable even. But this is over. It's been over for a long time. Now, do what you should have done and get out of here. Never let me see you again."

Felix nodded to a guard who untied the man with the loud voice. He stood to his feet, pausing to glance at Felix briefly as he dusted himself off and prepared to walk away. Without a word, he disappeared into the distance.

"He'll only come back for you," Equill said. "You should have killed him."

Felix shrugged. "He'll forget who he is soon enough," he said. "It really doesn't take long."

The King sighed. He approached the crows with a look of sadness. He nodded suddenly, the words of the guard echoing in his ears. He fell to his knees, Jalopy put his crown at his feet, and he looked up slowly to meet the eyes of the crow.

"Very well," he said. "You win."

"No," said Mitto. "No one has to lose."

REBUILDING THE CAVERNS

THE NEWS SPREAD QUICKLY AMONG THE PEOPLE. Guards and soldiers put down their weapons and started giving the food hidden deep in the walls of the tower to the starving and the weak — mere afterthoughts of Jalopy only short days before. Carba, Cevec and Safil joined with the people and the territory was understood as an extension of the crow village. Though it was never declared as such, the people and the crows migrated to and from the two locations freely as time and circumstance determined necessary. For most purposes, the two were considered a unified location with no clear boundary between them.

Jalopy was reluctant until he heard back from the peasants he had left behind in his homeland. In a letter overjoyed by the news of the caverns' transformation, far from the chaos he had imagined, a time of merry rebirth was described. The letter softened his anxieties and assured him to join the people in organizing the crows' various scavenging findings. Soon, the people who had once lived in his kingdom started to join the caverns and invite the inhabitants below to join them above.

Gwan and Mitto opened a community centre so that people and crows could work without fear of the children. Equill used the former prison to explain right and wrong to those who created problems in the community. Though the conversation was often heated, she always succeeded in making them understand. Every meeting ended with the shaking of hands and the end of the tensions that had brought them to her.

The spider kept the bad dreams at bay during the night. During the day, she went where she was needed, either sharing good stories so they would sleep easier or offering her help where needed. When she announced that she had a litter of eggs coming, everyone decided that she should keep the history of the cavern and pass it on to her children so that all below the caverns would know the history that was now shared. She taught several of the crows how to bind bad dreams so that they could continue the task when she or her children were asleep. After a slow period of learning — during which many of the crows became trapped in the webs — they were able to keep the bad dreams bound with webs made from the silk of plants from the surface.

Felix sat at the side, watching intently but deciding that it was best to let the people and the crows determine how to rebuild. With the sight, he could see the foundations of the people's former dwelling grow stronger. When asked, he would lend a hand with the organization and rationing of the crows' findings and he never wore an expression without a grin.

The man with the loud voice was largely forgotten, except as the punchline of jokes passed along as people worked.

Only the serpent was absent. It wasn't until a few weeks had passed that she returned. She found Felix overlooking a scene of celebration one night.

"You did well, Felix," she said. "But the time has come for you to return the sight and go to the surface once again."

Felix was tempted to protest — he had grown attached to the caverns — but he agreed that it was for the best. He looked around at every crevice and every curve of the scene before him, using the sight one last time to absorb the kind atmosphere. Then, he followed the serpent to the fountain.

He closed his eyes as the fountain swept the water from his eyes.

When he opened them again, he saw only what was immediately obvious. He could imagine the small details that had been inescapable — the source of first pain and then knowledge — through the sight, but he could no longer see them plainly.

"I am honoured," Felix said. "Not many have the chance to see the world in this way. Why did you choose me? Surely there was some reason that I, of all people, fell into the pit."

"Every crow is given the sight when they become an adolescent and must return it when they become an adult," the stone serpent said as they returned to the celebration. "Remember that and you will be able to defeat the blond beast."

"Am I to kill it?" Felix asked.

"No," replied the stone serpent. "You can't kill the blond beast — you can only move past it. In time as others defeat it, those woods it lurks in will become smaller and smaller until it is left to stalk around a single tree. But when that day finally comes, no one will ever have to pay the blond beast any mind again. When those days finally come, the blond beast will be dead in every sense that matters. But you can only contribute, Felix. You cannot do all of that on your own."

Felix nodded. The crows told him to go into the mists and to keep walking. He looked back to see Jalopy engaged in conversation with the spider. He wore a smile that appeared foreign to his cheeks. The spider wore a look of friendly interest and nodded enthusiastically as she listened. Behind the conversation, some crows played with Jalopy's children as people milled about the village, helping the crows with the daily toils as if they had been born there.

The sight had left his eyes, but even in its absence, he could see the bright future that the village was creating for all who dwelt there.

Felix walked slowly into the mists. As they rose, they engulfed him and he kept walking, closing his eyes as he guided his feet forward. He opened them again and watched as the mists faded into the grasses and the open skies of the flat plains.

He blinked, setting his hand against the sun to block its rays from his adjusting eyes. He never stopped walking, even as the woods ahead emerged from the horizon. Felix entered the shade of the trees.

The shadows they cast over the floor of the forest struck him as a mild comfort compared to the unceasing heat of the sun outside.

This time, as he pushed his feet forward, he had a destination in mind. For the first time since he could recall, he was confident with where he was going. He thought suddenly of the shame that had been in his heart as he had wandered aimlessly before. Now that shame seemed more distant than any hamlet he had ever stopped in before. Finally, when his thoughts turned again to Cuthbert, he felt a longing but no longer any guilt — Felix finally felt his mind at ease.

He bent down and picked some bittercress billowing in the wind beside him. He ate the plant with a tear in his eye. He had forgotten how much he liked the taste.

THE BLOND BEAST

FELIX CREPT INTO THE FOREST, his pace remaining steady as he watched the leaves above. The dancing shapes from the canopy of the trees laid a path before him. As he walked, Felix's eyes fell upon the bones and corpses that littered the forest floor — he had made it further into the woods than he ever had before. He kept walking and followed the path to a blood-soaked clearing where he sat and waited.

He remained still, watching the sunlight. He leaned back upon a tree stump behind him and nearly drifted into a sleep. Felix was only awoken by the sound of a rhythmic breath. When he looked up, he saw a shadow cast over the woods. The blond beast stood before him, licking its chops as it inhaled his scent.

Felix stood up, slowly and let his glance sink into the beast's bright, blue eyes. The blond beast took a long, bony hand and swept back the sparse quills of yellow hair on its head. The sun shone yellow over the mahogany clothes that covered its body as it stood still.

"Albert Gould," he said slowly, scanning the beast as he recalled the tale. "Your name was Albert Gould. You were a man once — before you were this. Do you remember that?"

The beast tilted its head as Felix spoke, its blank eyes scanning him.

"Do you remember what it is to be human? Can you remember what it's like to laugh or to cry? Is there any part of you left, Albert? If I stayed in that town, would I have ended up like you — a sad husk of nothing?"

The beast remained silent, snarling as it studied Felix a moment longer. Felix let a warning burn in his eyes. He sent a deliberate glare to the tall trees on the plains and then looked back into the beast's vision. He took a step forward, dropping his empty hands to his sides.

The beast watched his hands in anticipation. Felix's fingers began to shake as he narrowed his eyes, keeping his glance shooting forward. His hands formed a fist, and he clenched his jaw.

The beast looked away as Felix kept his eyes still. It began to pace around the perimeter of the clearing, mumbling in that same condescending gibberish. Then it stood, hanging its mouth open and letting the sun glint on its white teeth. The glance from the beast told Felix that he was expected to understand whatever had been said. He only continued his glare. He did not understand, and he did not care. The beast began bobbing its head up and down rapidly. It let out a guttural snicker as it paced back to its original place. Through a crooked grin it began panting again.

Felix took another step forward. The beast answered by stepping into the light. He had seen its face before, but now, various scars — presumably from other encounters — glistened in the sunlight. The remnants of previous battle injuries suggested that the beast had lost before — that there were others beyond the trees. He let out a smirk to match the beast's crooked grin.

Then its grin pursed shut in rage, its brow furrowed. The beast charged, holding a foul, decorous blade above its head. The blade was clenched behind its wrist, ready to sink itself deep into Felix's chest.

As the strike of the charge neared, Felix reached out his hand to grab the beast's wrist. He wanted to stand above the beast in combat, but he could only step aside, turning his back foot outward and toward the coming threat. He felt the beast's foot stop suddenly over his ankle. It fell over his outstretched limb and tumbled forward. He turned to see its chin collide with the stump.

The beast's hideous blue eyes were forced shut by the pain as its pale flesh scraped against the wood. Its hands fell open and flat as its body landed in a heap, turning to the side under the force of the fall. The beast lay motionless, save for its subtle breathing.

The knife had dropped to the ground during its fall. Felix picked it up and held it into the light. He looked at the blond beast as it lay unconscious, and he knelt beside it. With all the force in his hands, he plunged the blade toward the beast's throat, only to find a strange resistant force in the air.

The force held the blade from the beast until Felix pushed against it.

He continued pressing until the blade finally fell into the beast's neck, sending flecks of blood shooting into the air. He caught his breath, only for it to flee once more as the beast convulsed and wheezed under the blade.

Felix jumped back. He recalled the words of the stone serpent as he froze in terror. The blade stood on end, protruding under the convulsing, enraged beast. The blow would have killed any other creature on earth, but the beast lived, only being held in place under its own blade. It reached for the hilt, trying at great might to free itself.

He stood up and walked away from the forest. Felix expected the beast to follow, but he was not followed as he walked to the edge of the trees. If the sound of breaking twigs had chased behind him, he would have fled, but in the silence, he kept his pace slow and calm. It seemed that the blow had knocked the blond beast into a slumber that it would not awake from soon.

When he saw the horizon on the other side of the trees, he felt a wave of relief wash over him, followed by an instinct of disbelief. He stopped to feel the sun of the opposite side wash over him as he stood still. When he felt the warmth touch his face, he walked forward. He looked back to see a tree beside him slowly sinking into the ground. The relief in Felix's heart left as he saw the blond beast running toward him. It stood, shouting like mad in its condescending gibberish and frolicking its arms in blind fury. Blood flowed from its throat as it struggled to move beyond the woods, only to be repelled by some unseen force that compelled it to remain.

Felix looked into the beast's eyes again. The fear in his heart was gone as he looked into its face — it was replaced with some new feeling. He was safe in the knowledge that the beast could no longer hurt him in exile. The horrible monster who had once seemed too strong to defeat was now rendered helpless and trapped in a hopeless struggle to gain the upper hand, even as its opponent was no longer engaged. He grinned, sending an enraged shriek from the blond beast as he turned and left.

As he walked on, Felix imagined the day when the woods would be reduced to a single tree. He felt the wind blow through him. He looked back a final time and saw the beast disappear into the depths of the wood, walking slowly under the pain of his fresh injury. The pain that had seemed so great before now seemed small, insignificant and the relic of a bygone point in his long journey forward.

The sun danced over the open blue sky, and Felix entered the flat plains once more. The sun's warmth — once a source of discomforted sweat — was a welcome touch upon his face as he felt the ground before him. When he became tired, he sat and rested until he felt his legs again. He looked around. There was no town in sight, even as he expected to find one in his tired delirium.

Felix stood up again and continued to walk, wondering where his feet would finally take him.

BEYOND THE FOREST

THE MONOTONY OF HIS JOURNEY LEFT FELIX at some point. Somewhere, Felix had expected to rediscover the repetition and the exhaustion that had been his only companions before, but it never appeared. In their place, he found something else. Every step he took felt so small against the ground below it, and he could only admire the landscape around him — in a landscape he once loathed, he now found appreciation. The rabbits were still jumping across the meadow. They stopped just before Felix's path to eat some of the grasses. He sat on the ground to watch them. As they ate, they moved over to make room for Felix. He smiled as he watched them, calmly observing until they hopped away into the distance.

Felix kept walking and looked above into the open sky. The blue was untouched by even the suggestion of a cloud. In the vacancy above, he saw the way the blue hue would shift with time, and the promise that eventually sheer billowing white clouds would come into view. They would accumulate, grow heavy with rain, and pour themselves out across the flat plains. The sky would clear, and the cycle would start again.

He kept walking, his eyes still in the sky as he went — the land was flat and posed no threat of obstacles ahead. When a long, thin smoke stream blew into view — resembling a snake in its shape — he looked down to find the buildings of a small town ahead.

As he walked through the streets, Felix felt as though he had seen the town before, even as his better sense reminded him that this was impossible. He looked around the houses, the general store and the bar. For reasons he could not explain, he knew where the buildings were. The town was small, but if he wanted to see a building, it was simply found just before his eyes.

The confusion in the atmosphere did not intimidate Felix — there was nothing malicious. Rather, it compelled him to walk further down the streets. Soon, some inhabitants emerged, and they watched him as he walked. They seemed only share his bewilderment — it was evident that outsiders rarely visited the town.

From one of the back alleys, a small sound came. Felix turned and saw a small black cat, meowing into the street. He knelt down to greet the cat and it approached and rubbed against his feet and then his hand as he reached out. The cat rolled happily on the ground as Felix stroked the creature's ears. A smile stretched over his face as a purr vibrated through the cat's throat and resounded in the soles of his feet. He turned to see the people of the town watching him with warm smiles.

"Well,," said an old woman with a sunspot as she approached Felix, "Heprer seems to like you. She doesn't seem to like anyone anymore. Maybe we've all become boring or something."

Felix grinned as the cat stood up and rubbed against his leg again before skipping away. "I just thought she was calling to me," Felix said, watching Heprer disappear behind a fence.

"She just appeared one day when she was a kitten," the old woman explained as the other townspeople went back to their business. "We gave her some milk, and we helped her along, but she never showed that kind of affection to anyone after she became an adult cat. Heprer keeps the rats and mice away, so we keep feeding her. I think she finds us strange, given that she is the only cat in the town. Perhaps we'll have to find some more."

The old woman's eyes widened with her sunspot, and she stepped forward, looking back to invite Felix to follow. The old woman chattered as they walked, gesturing emphatically to the various houses and buildings that flanked the singular street of the town. She led him to a park bench near a fountain in the middle of the town where they sat.

The fountain's water was murky as it spouted from the pipes, but it became clear as it settled in the small puddle around the perimeter.

"And you?" the old woman suddenly asked. The question had come after a long-winded history of the town that had fallen empty upon Felix's distracted ears. He looked to the ground, unsure of how best to respond.

"I came here from the forest," he responded.

"Ah, yes," replied the old woman. "Forgive me for saying this, but I think we've met before, young man."

Felix nodded. "I remember. I spoke to so many people on the road. I'd never forget how you fed me that once."

The woman smiled.

"I knew it wasn't a mistake to believe in you," she said.

They walked further down the streets, watching as people went about their business.

"The first people here faced that beast," the old woman continued. "Their actions are the only reason that we're here now. Those woods used to be so great that they began to disrupt the bushes and the trees where the founders of this place found their food. So, they went through it and they found more food on the other side. We live quite well here, you see. And now that the woods are shrinking, we might be able to go back one day and find those of us whose ancestors did not go on that journey. Well, not in my lifetime of course."

The old woman laughed and Felix nodded, slowly with a smile. He turned to the forest — it was still visible from the town. He tried to imagine the woods being any greater — they looked smaller than they had when he had first crossed, but they were still so wide that they encompassed his entire vision.

"My name is Maskwa, by the way."

The old woman explained in a tone that expected an answer.

When Maskwa received no reply, she sighed and suggested that Felix find something to eat. He nodded and followed the old woman to the nearby bar. It was barely occupied — built to house more people than lived in the town — and the few patrons had an eased view of the two as they entered.

The barkeep looked up from wiping down a table. She poured Maskwa a glass of water, studying Felix carefully. With a shrug, she Felix what he would have.

"Whatever there is," Felix answered.

The barkeep nodded and handed Felix a glass of strange, pink liquid. "This is radish juice," she explained. "It's a fairly common drink around here, but I understand if it's too strong."

Felix shook his head and drank the liquid. He expected to find the taste disagreeing with his tongue, but it didn't bother him. He thanked the barkeep and began fishing in his pockets. When he found nothing but cloth, he turned to Maskwa.

"I have no money," he said, worriedly. "I'd hate to make you pay for me."

"Money," Maskwa said back. "It's been a long time since I've heard that word. No, you don't have to put a dirty piece of metal on the counter for your drink. We have a different way of paying each other back around here — we support one another. Tell me who you are. I'm curious."

Felix shrugged.

"I'm not sure," he said. "I forgot who I was for a long time but now that I remember, it all seems so distant — whoever I was then, I'm someone totally different now."

Maskwa sat in silence but her eyes suggested her thoughts. The barkeep handed them each a plate of rice with some corn of various colours on the side.

"This has always impressed me," Maskwa said, holding up the red, yellow and blue corn with a grin. "We changed the roots in the crops and now we can make whatever kind of corn we like. Just as long as we are gentle, and we remember to be nothing but the guide of the soil, the corn is always good. It's strange. I've seen this every day since I was a kid, but I can't help being amazed. The more I think about it, the more I realize what a miracle the corn is and how lucky we are to be eating it.

"This soil isn't like the soil on the other side of those woods — there, the dirt was good, and it grew everything we needed just as long as we left it alone, but here it won't grow anything unless we plant it. The soil over there was ruined because the people couldn't understand why it was best to leave it alone. Here, we have no choice if we're going to eat. It's strange, but what didn't make sense there makes perfect sense here.

"Different lands, different soils, different ways of being, you see — and it's our job to listen and to understand which is best. That is what it means to live well. We are the land. If we are respectful and we make a way of life that understands the world, we will always live long and healthy lives. Do you know how old I am, young man?"

Felix shook his head.

"I am one hundred and eighty-one years old — the first eighty of those were lived on those flat plains because I knew how to live on that land. The people around me knew as well and some of my grandparents lived to be even older. My great-grandfather — when he was my great-grandmother — lived to be a hundred ninety-five, and then she was my great-grandmother, and she lived for eleven more years afterwards."

Felix smiled shyly as he ate the meal before him. He stared out at the landscape — a glint of the flat plains was visible through the trees of the woods in the distance — and he felt embarrassed at himself for ever thinking they couldn't support life.

He looked down at the food in front of him. It seemed small on the plate, but as he finished it, he felt full and ready to begin walking again. He started to stand up, only to feel compelled to remain sitting with Maskwa.

"Well," she said, putting down her glass, "if you want to know how we return favours, let me show you. Hey, Ayamis, what do you need done?"

The barkeep turned and paused a moment to think.

"Let me see," she said, tapping her finger in thought. "The crops outside could use some attention and we could always use some more wood — winter will be here in just a few months."

Maskwa nodded and turned back to Felix.

"This is how you pay for things here," she explained. "Ayamis made you a good meal and a drink, now you go and look after her crops, or you can gather wood. Whatever you don't pick is left for me — I ate too. This was good food, you see, not the simple roots and berries we eat to keep from starving. This food was prepared deliberately for us, so now we help Ayamis."

Felix chose to gather wood, as he assumed that it would be less work for the old woman to tend to the crops. Ayamis thanked them as they left and soon Felix was out in the flat plains once more. Only now, he had a clear purpose for being there.

"Only the dead wood," Maskwa instructed. "Anything green can be grown so that we can use it later."

Felix nodded and he began to place the pieces of fallen wood from the sparse trees into the little basket they had given him. Even in the absence of the sight, he found himself observing each piece of wood for signs of green — examining every part of it carefully before he determined that it was good to be burned. He left wood behind at even the first sign of green.

The basket filled slowly at first — only a small amount of the fallen wood was completely dead and trees were rare on the flat plains. Felix was tempted to go to the woods behind him, only deciding to refrain from entering as he recalled the blond beast. He wondered what the beast did when it wasn't stalking its prey. Without the sight, he could only speculate. He put some more wood into the basket and turned away, letting the beast fade from his thoughts. As he turned away from the woods, they seemed smaller and less daunting than before. With the basket full, Felix stood up and slowly walked back to the village.

He met Ayamis on the way, carrying a tray full of drinks as she went. She said that she was picking up a few more stools from the woodworkers after a few had been broken some weeks before. Felix asked if he could come and she agreed, letting him drop off the basket at the bar before rejoining her.

She took him to a small shed occupied by workers who sat, sawing and hammering various pieces of wood into shapes of benches, tables and chairs. A smiling man greeted Ayamis and handed her a number of carved stools. In response, she put the tray on the floor. Each of the workers took a glass of water from the tray before returning to work.

"Isn't that it?" Felix asked when Ayamis did not leave. "Didn't you pay them for the stools just now?"

"No," Ayamis replied, concealing her desire to join the workers' laughter under a smile. "I was just giving them what they need — it's a hot day and they've been working, so I gave them water. I repay them with carefully prepared meals and drinks in the bar. But we always make sure everyone gets what they need to live."

"What in the hell?" called one of the workers suddenly, making Ayamis and Felix jump. Felix turned to see a worker sitting at the table with a bullmastiff at his feet. The worker stood to his feet and ran toward Felix excitedly.

"I thought you were dead, kid," Holsapple said, his face returning slowly to Felix's memory. "Everyone else from Doufsie is — well apart from Carla Welwood. She's around here somewhere but she won't talk to me. Can't say I don't get it." Holsapple turned to the ground and sighed.

"I just made it out because of that guy I arrested — I don't know his name — he was fighting that lunatic and I had time to get out of there. I guess I wasn't the only one after all. It's so much better here — I wish everyone in Doufsie could just come here and see that things could have been so much better than they were back home. I'm so happy you're here, kid."

"Cuthbert," Felix replied. "His name was Cuthbert Kahmekwaskawew. He was a friend of mine."

"Thanks," Holsapple replied with a nod. "Tell me about him sometime. I've been wondering about the man who saved my life — our lives. Now I know he probably didn't do it for us. He certainly didn't do it for me — I mean, I wouldn't have — but I'm still glad he was there anyway. It gave me just enough time to get out. I made a lot of mistakes in my life, Felix. Too many to count. But because of that man — your friend — I have a chance at starting again and getting it right this time. I won't pretend to know why I got this chance, but I have it. Life is fragile — you can't waste it."

Holsapple turned over a small stool and whittled a shape into it. "His name," he said. "How do you spell it?"

Felix felt a strange joy in his heart as he spoke the letters — he didn't expect to see Holsapple but even stranger was the fact that he was glad to see him alive. Holsapple shook away his large grin and turned to Ayamis, who stood patiently waiting behind the bar.

"Sorry, kid. Didn't mean to interrupt. I'll catch you around," he nodded and Ayamis took him back to the bar.

"It's good Dominic will have someone to help him out. He's a good guy, really, and he tries. I just think he's having a hard time adjusting to life here. I don't think he's used to living with people who aren't out to get him."

"It's funny," Felix said with a smile. "The last time I saw him, he tried to feed me to his dog."

"People are strange, aren't we?" Ayamis responded, turning back to the bar. "Very, very strange. We don't even make sense to ourselves."

Just outside, Maskwa stood over a garden, gently watering some crops. She looked up with a grin and motioned for Felix to join him.

"I have to get these crops ready for winter," Maskwa said. "The wood you gathered will help us too."

Felix smiled as Ayamis said her thanks. Maskwa took him to a small house at the edge of the town. It was a hovel with two rooms — a bathroom beside a larger room with a bed, a sofa and a stove. To Felix, the house seemed modest compared to where he had lived with his parents in the city, but somehow, it was more comfortable.

The old woman went to the stove and explained how to use it as she boiled a kettle for tea. "You can stay here if you like," Maskwa explained. "For no reason other than you seem to have nowhere to go, and you look like you could use somewhere safe to live — that's what we all deserve, you know."

Felix nodded, thanking the old woman with a softened glance. He sat on the bed, looking over the room.

"Though I do have to ask," Maskwa said, suddenly pouring the tea into two metal cups, "who are you? I know that you are a good person, but you can't be a stranger in the town here. Dominic knows you but don't we all deserve that courtesy?"

Felix nodded, taking a cup of tea as Maskwa handed it to him. He sat still, holding the warmth in his hands as he lulled a thought into his mind.

"My name is Felix August Cabil Babimoosay," he said plainly. "The rest remains to be seen."

"Welcome home." Maskwa said with a knowing smirk fading as she stepped back to the town.

ACKNOWLEDGEMENTS

I would like to thank my supportive family; my father Bob, my mother, Tady, my siblings Riel and Polaris, my grandparents, Don, Marion and Lynn, my uncle John, my cousins Caileigh and Abbe; my amazing editor, Jazz Cook; the generous editor of my first book of short stories, Jason Eaglespeaker; my helpful and patient friends, William Bessai-Saul, Kye Rajaraman, Kyle Bauld, Seb Reade, Catriona Profit, Clementine Alexandria Ball, Emma Wheaton, Carole Kowcun, Michelle Robinson, Lourdes Curaçao, Jonathan Ouellette, Francine Blyant and many others who prefer to remain anonymous; my writing instructors, Gail Sobat, Basil Rose and Christopher Donohoe; and everyone else who inspired and supported me in completing this work. Thank you for reading early drafts, helping me to overcome writer's block and for offering guidance and encouragement where necessary. I am grateful to have such a great network of support in you all.